EXCALIBUR

SENTINEL SECURITY #5

ANNA HACKETT

Excalibur

Published by Anna Hackett

Copyright 2023 by Anna Hackett

Cover by Mayhem Cover Creations

Cover image by FuriousFotog/Golden Czermak

Edits by Tanya Saari

ISBN (ebook): 978-1-922414-80-9

ISBN (paperback): 978-1-922414-81-6

At Star's End – One of Library Journal's Best E-Original Romances for 2014

The Phoenix Adventures – SFR Galaxy Award Winner for Most Fun New Series and "Why Isn't This a Movie?" Series

Beneath a Trojan Moon – SFR Galaxy Award Winner and RWAus Ella Award Winner

Hell Squad – SFR Galaxy Award for best Post-Apocalypse for Readers who don't like Post-Apocalypse

Sign up for my VIP mailing list and get your *free box set* containing three action-packed romances.

Visit here to get started: www.annahackett.com

CHAPTER ONE

A*ddie.*

It was *his* Addie.

Bram O'Donovan stared across the busy Irish bar, his gaze on the woman who'd haunted his dreams for months.

She is not yours, you eejit.

No. Not his. But...they'd spent ten days together. For ten days, he'd gorged himself on her.

He'd thought...

Well, it didn't matter what he'd thought. Adaline Harris was young, blonde, beautiful, an amazing dancer, and sweet. She was too good for him.

He was an older, battered, ex-military man who would never be good enough for her. While he'd been away with work, she'd wised up.

He barely registered the sounds of the people in the bar. Addie looked up and met his gaze, and all the color drained out of her face, leaving her whiter than the sheets his ma used to have flapping outside on the line when he was a boy.

That's when his brain registered that Addie wore the uniform of the staff at the bar—black shirt and pants, and a dark-green apron.

And that apron sat snug over a small mound of a belly that she hadn't possessed the last time he'd seen her.

Shock rocketed through him.

Addie was pregnant.

She whirled and ran behind the bar, disappearing through a doorway.

Pregnant. It'd been several months since she'd disappeared from his life. He'd returned home to find she'd left her dance show and her apartment, and her phone had been disconnected.

That baby in her belly was his.

His friends at the table where he sat had fallen silent. Without a word, he rose and strode after Addie. He shouldered past several bargoers.

"Hey." One man spun around, took in Bram's size, and snapped his mouth closed.

Bram charged around the bar and through the door, ignoring a shout behind him.

Where was she?

There were several rooms off a long hallway. He heard the noise of the kitchen nearby. Then he detected the faint scent of spring flowers. It made him think of a sunny meadow. Her scent was embedded in his senses. He'd know it anywhere. He'd damn well dreamed about it over the last few months.

Addie.

He stalked to a door at the end of the hall and nudged it open.

It was filled with stacked tables, St. Patrick's Day decorations, and racks of unused glasses.

Addie stood in the center of the space, and spun to face him.

"Addie," he murmured.

She swallowed. "Bram, I..."

"You disappeared," he said.

Her head jerked. Her blonde hair was up in a jumbled bun on top of her head. It always made him think of strands of golden sunshine.

She lifted her chin. "You wanted nothing to do with us." She placed a protective hand over her belly.

His mind boiled. *Nothing to do with her? Feck.*

There was a baby in there. *His* baby.

Confusion made him cock his head. "You disappeared, Addie. I thought it was a pretty clear way of telling me you didn't want me. A baby..." He scraped a hand through his short hair. "I had a right to know about that."

Splotches of color appeared on her cheeks. "I called. I tried to get in touch. I left you messages."

His brows drew together. "I didn't get any messages."

"I called Sentinel Security. And I went there. *Twice.*" The color left her cheeks again, the look in her eyes stark. "I was told to stop bothering you. I got the message, Bram." Her voice hitched.

His gut knotted. "I don't know what you're talking about."

"Just leave me alone." She grabbed the edge of the

table. Her knuckles were white. "I've been doing just fine on my own."

The pain and hurt in her voice cut him. His throat was as dry as dust. He couldn't handle the idea of her alone. "You left the show."

"Show?" She frowned at him.

"*On the Street*. Where you were dancing."

She gave a short laugh. "I'm pregnant, Bram. No one wants a pregnant dancer."

"Addie—"

"And I was sick for a while."

His own stomach cramped at the thought.

"I couldn't afford my apartment anymore! I couldn't find any work, and I was puking constantly."

His body jerked. He hadn't meant to, but he'd left her all alone.

"I couldn't even pay for my phone." She lifted her chin. "I was lucky Paddy took me on here."

"I didn't get your messages, sunshine."

If it was possible, her cheeks went even paler. "Don't call me that," she whispered.

He'd called her that during the nights they'd spent together. Wrapped up together in her small double bed, where there had barely been enough room for him, let alone both of them. But he'd held her tight. He'd learned every inch of that beautiful dancer's body. He'd cherished pleasing her, hearing her cries as she'd come for him.

Now there was so much pain in her pretty, blue eyes, and he was desperate to fix it.

She rubbed both hands over her belly.

"Addie, come with me. We need to talk."

"I'm at work, I—"

"I'm not leaving you alone." Not again. A part of Bram panicked at the thought of leaving her, worried he'd lose her.

She wasn't disappearing from his life again.

"Bram, I think it's best you go." Her voice wobbled.

"No," he growled.

Her lips pressed together. Addie was kind and good, but he knew she had an inner strength when things were important to her. She could dig her heels in.

"Bram?" His boss Killian's voice sounded behind him.

"I think she needs some time, Bram. You both do." That voice belonged to Devyn, Killian's new, badass wife. For some reason, the stubborn CIA agent had claimed Bram as a friend.

He turned his head and met her gaze. The redhead nodded at him.

Bram hadn't known Devyn long, but he knew she'd have his back. They'd saved each other's lives on a recent mission. He released a breath and looked back at Addie, who was staring at Devyn.

"Addie?" he said.

Her head jerked back to him, a strange look on her face.

He frowned. "Sunshine?"

Her mouth opened, but then her legs collapsed, and she started to fall.

Bram had never moved so fast in his life. He lunged across the room to catch her.

ADDIE BLINKED OPEN HER EYES, fighting the grogginess in her head.

Strong arms held her, and a part of her just wanted to snuggle into them. It felt nice to be held. It was nice to lean on someone else.

She'd been alone a long time. Ever since she'd left that tiny house belonging to her parents in Hickory Ridge, Georgia. She loved her parents, even when they could be distant and unsupportive. They were always too worn down and tired, and had been her entire life. They'd both worked and had six kids to feed. Her father worked at a factory, and drank too much. Her mom worked two jobs and was always exhausted.

Addie had learned that her mother had wanted to be a singer when she'd been younger. Once, Addie had caught her mom singing as she'd folded laundry. She had a beautiful voice, and Addie had told her. But her mom had clammed up and snapped at her.

When your father put you in my belly, my life, my dream, was over. Never trust a man, Adaline. Only trust yourself.

Shirley Harris had given up her dream.

Addie had wanted more than that. More than a rundown house, threadbare clothes, and constant tiredness.

She'd wanted to make something of herself. She hadn't been the most amazing student at school, but she'd been good at computers and dancing. She'd decided to make it as a dancer.

And secretly, she'd always wanted a man who'd love her.

Not a perfect prince. She wanted a solid, trustworthy man, who looked at her like she was the most precious thing in the world.

Her mother had told her that she was an idiot with her head in the clouds, and bound for disappointment.

Addie was *never* going to believe that.

She snuggled against a hard chest. A *very* hard chest.

Memories stabbed at her.

Of a powerfully strong body, a rugged face, sexy red hair, and big hands touching her with desperate need.

Bram.

She could even smell him now. Leather and spice.

No. Bram had left her. Bram didn't want her.

Pain cut at her. She'd already cried too many tears for the quiet Irishman who'd broken her heart. Bram was gone.

She opened her eyes and stared into green ones.

Bram.

Her heart squeezed. He was holding her.

"God, sunshine, are you okay?" His voice was a deep rumble with that accent she loved.

"I—" She shifted, and her head swam. She let out a low moan.

She saw panic flare in his eyes before he hid it.

No, that couldn't be right. Bram was solid and unshakable as a rock. Nothing panicked him.

"She needs a doctor." He rose with her in his arms. "Don't move, Addie. Take it easy."

Addie wasn't small. She was tall, but he lifted her like she weighed nothing.

Then, she noticed the healing bruises on his face. They circled his eye, and there was a bandage at his temple. Her fingers reached up to touch him.

"You're hurt," she murmured.

"It's nothing," he mumbled.

It didn't look like nothing. A part of her hated the idea of him injured.

"She needs a doctor," he said again. "Get Daniel. I'm taking her back to the Sentinel Security warehouse."

She realized that he was talking to the other two people in the room.

Addie tried to think. She couldn't leave. "I'm work—"

"Shh, Addie. We'll get you checked first."

Her head was fuzzy, and she felt faint. She thought it best not to tell him about the wave of nausea rushing over her.

The worst of her morning sickness had passed, thank the stars, but every now and then, she did feel unsteady.

"What's going on here?"

The deep, raspy voice belonged to her new boss. Paddy Ryan was Irish-American through and through. He took great pride in his newest Irish bar, On the Rocks. He'd taken her on when no one else would. She tried to straighten in Bram's arms.

But Bram's hold tightened, and she was distracted by the way his huge biceps strained against his white shirt. He gently set her down, but kept his arms around her.

"Addie fainted," Bram said. "I'm taking her to get checked by a doctor."

"Paddy, I'm fine," she rushed to assure her boss.

Paddy stood in the doorway with his arms crossed. He was in his early sixties, with gray hair, and a scruffy gray beard. "You always say that, even when you're not."

She huffed out a breath. "That's not true."

"Yes, it is." Paddy's gaze never left Bram. "And who are you?" her boss demanded.

"We're friends of Addie's," the stunning, redheaded woman said. She shot Paddy a dazzling smile.

"As far as I know, she doesn't have any friends." Paddy scowled. "She's alone and pregnant."

Again, Addie felt Bram's arms convulse.

"We were out of the country," Killian said. "Bram's been looking for Addie, but she'd left her apartment, and her phone was disconnected."

The words echoed in her head. Bram had been looking for her? That couldn't be right.

She focused on Killian Hawke. He was dressed in an expensive, dark-blue suit but still managed to look dangerous. She'd met her friend Saskia Hawke's brother a couple of times before. Saskia had been one of the country's best ballerinas, but she'd recently retired to start her own school.

Saskia and Addie had become friends in the worst of circumstances—when a wealthy Russian businessman had become obsessed with Saskia and had her abducted. Of course, Addie had been in the wrong place at the wrong time, and gotten snatched as well. It had been terrifying. Her throat tightened.

Thankfully, Killian loved his sister and had used his resources to rescue her, Addie, and the other women who'd been kept by Yaroslav Mikhailov. To be honest, Killian scared Addie. She knew he was ex-CIA, and now owned a private security company, Sentinel Security. That was where Bram worked.

She assumed the beautiful redhead worked at Sentinel Security, too. She wore stylish wide-legged dark-green pants and a fitted black shirt tucked into them. Addie couldn't tuck her shirts in anymore, and the woman suddenly made her feel very dowdy. The way the redhead and Bram had looked at each other...it was clear they were close.

Addie's stomach took an unhappy nosedive. Was this woman his girlfriend?

Suddenly Bram, who was glaring at Paddy, slid a huge palm over her belly. She gasped at the sensation. Her body remembered just how those big, scarred hands had touched her.

When she'd first found out she was pregnant, she'd dreamed of Bram touching her belly, talking to their baby. Those dreams had withered and died.

"I'm the father of the baby," Bram said.

At this, Paddy's face darkened. The older man was not afraid of letting his temper loose. "Then why the fuck was she alone in the first place?"

Addie held out a hand. "Paddy—"

"She was bloody desperate when she came in here. No money for rent. No one to help her."

Another wave of dizziness hit her, and she slumped back against Bram's chest.

He made a growling sound and pulled her closer. "She needs a doctor." He lifted her into his arms again, without a single sign of strain, then shouldered toward the door.

"Bram, I'll be fine." She didn't want to go with him. Being around him hurt too much.

A muscle in his jaw flexed. "I'm going to make sure you're okay." His gaze flicked to her belly, an unreadable look in his green eyes.

"We have an excellent doctor on staff," Killian said to Paddy. "We'll take good care of her."

Paddy frowned, finally taking a good look at Killian. "You're Killian Hawke."

"I am. Bram works for me."

The bar owner sniffed. "Then I couldn't stop you taking her if I tried."

Killian's sharp face was cool and composed. "We have Adaline's best interests at heart."

Addie just closed her eyes. Bram had wanted nothing to do with her and the baby. He'd made that obvious.

But when she told him she'd left him messages, he'd looked so confused.

She squeezed her eyes closed harder. Her brain was too foggy to think right now.

Bram walked out of the room, holding her tight.

"I'm going to take care of you, I promise," he said.

She wanted that to be true, but her heart was too broken to believe him.

CHAPTER TWO

Bram sat and watched as the Sentinel Security doctor, Dr. Daniel Chu, checked Addie over.

She sat in a chair in the kitchen area of the office. Sentinel Security was a large organization, and the upper levels of the warehouse were home to the corporate and cybersecurity teams.

Down here in the lower levels was where Killian's alpha team worked. They were all former military and international law enforcement, with the skills to carry out more complex and dangerous jobs.

After years in the Irish Army Ranger Wing and Directorate of Military Intelligence, Bram had been looking for a change, and Killian had approached him.

There'd been nothing for him in Ireland, except his dad—a bitter, cranky, old man. Bram saw him once a year, and that was enough for the both of them.

Bram liked working for Sentinel Security. It suited him. Usually, he could work behind the scenes, and he avoided personal protection. He preferred not dealing with people unless he had to.

Killian had renovated an old cargo warehouse to house the Sentinel Security offices. He'd kept the brick walls and black iron touches, but the rest of the place was accented with modern décor, and lots of greenery.

All the main Sentinel Security team had apartments on the upper levels. It made for a short commute to the office, which Bram liked a lot. He hated the New York traffic.

As the slim, dark-haired Daniel murmured to Addie, Bram couldn't take his eyes off her. She had some color back in her cheeks, and now she glowed. Her hair was thick and golden, her breasts a little fuller. He shifted in his chair, feeling a shot of guilt about feeling a definite twitch in his cock.

She's pregnant, you feck.

Daniel strapped a blood pressure cuff on her arm. "So, are you taking prenatal vitamins? Sleeping okay?"

Addie nodded. "Mostly. My feet ache sometimes, and I can't always find a comfy position to sleep in."

"That's all normal, and probably only going to get more challenging," Daniel said.

She pulled a face. "Great." Then she smiled. "Actually, I can't wait. Even the not-so-fun things, like morning sickness, have been an experience. I just want to soak it all up."

The doctor smiled at her. "And how far along are you?"

"Eighteen weeks." She flicked a glance at Bram.

Which time had gotten her pregnant? He'd used

condoms, but he knew they weren't one hundred percent effective. Plus once or twice, he'd been too far gone and slid into her without protection. He'd finally pulled out and suited up, but...

The image of her beneath him bloomed in his head. Her crying out for him to go deeper.

Fuck. He shifted, trying to hide his growing erection.

Daniel glanced at him, and Bram kept his gaze on the green wall in the kitchen area.

"You're showing quite a bit, considering this is your first pregnancy. Did your OB-GYN do an ultrasound?"

"Yes. At ten weeks. I told her that the father was tall and big." Another glance at Bram.

"Blood pressure is good." Daniel smiled. "When was the last time you ate?"

She licked her lips. "Lunch. I was busy and running late for work. I forgot."

Bram leaned forward and his chair creaked. She wasn't looking after herself. He'd change that.

"And I'd say you got a bit of a shock seeing the big guy here," Daniel said. "So feeling a little dizzy is normal considering. Make sure you eat regularly. With Bram's genes, I'm guessing this baby will be a good size."

Bram felt a jolt of shock. Suddenly it hit him that the child growing inside her was from him. He blinked.

"Are you going to find out the sex of the baby?" Daniel asked.

"Um, I'm not sure. I have an ultrasound scheduled in a few days." She glanced at Bram nervously. "I wasn't even sure I wanted to find out. I'll love this baby either way." Her voice took on a fierce edge.

"Bram, get her some juice, and see if we have any decent snacks left in the kitchen," Daniel said.

"I'll get it." Hex rounded the corner and headed for the fridge, tossing them a smile.

Daniel rolled his dark eyes. "Eavesdropping, Hex?"

The tiny, dark-haired guru of all things tech at Sentinel Security turned and grinned. "Hello, I'm a hacker, remember? I know everything." The lights caught on the pink streaks at the bottom of her hair. She grabbed a small bottle of juice and a granola bar, and smiled at Addie. "Hi, I'm Jet, but everyone around here calls me Hex."

"Hi. I'm Adaline, but most people call me Addie." Addie tilted her head. "You have one blue eye and one green."

"I do. I'm one of a kind."

"Sorry." Addie waved a hand. "I'm always blurting things out. Your eyes are pretty."

Hex smiled. "Thanks. Saskia's mentioned you." Hex handed the drink and bar over. "Plus Bram here gave me your details when he asked me to track you down."

Addie froze. "He did?"

Hex just smiled and nodded.

As Addie sipped her drink, Bram fought the urge to haul her into his arms.

"Okay, if you need anything else, you just call." Daniel stood, and met Bram's gaze.

He nodded at the doctor. Then he turned to Hex. "Hex, Addie said she called the Sentinel Security office and left me messages. She also called my cellphone. I never got anything."

The hacker frowned, toying with the pink ends of her hair. "You talked to someone in reception upstairs?"

Addie nodded. "A woman. I tried his cellphone and left messages. It just beeped."

"All the cellphones are redirected to the office when the guys are out of the country. Only approved numbers get through." Hex frowned. "You still should've gotten her messages."

"I came into the office as well," Addie said. "The woman upstairs...was very polite. The first two times she told me Bram was unavailable. The third time—" Addie looked down at her lap "—she told me it was time to stop embarrassing myself."

Bram growled, got out of his chair, and knelt by Addie. He grabbed her hand. "I swear I didn't know."

"I'll look into this," Hex murmured, before she left them alone.

He stroked the soft skin at Addie's wrist. "I looked for you when I got back."

He'd been desperate to see her. He'd even bought her flowers—beautiful yellow roses. They'd reminded him of Addie's happy personality. He'd never met anyone who could always see the positive in everything like her.

"You'd left your apartment, your phone was disconnected. I looked for you at your show." He looked down at the floor. He remembered that after realizing she was gone, he'd tossed the flowers in a dumpster. "I figured you didn't want to see me. You knew where to find me, and I thought you'd come to your senses and weren't interested."

"Bram—"

He looked up. She was biting her lip.

"I was so afraid when I found out I was pregnant, then I was excited thinking about the baby, then I was terrified when I couldn't reach you. I figured you'd gotten what you wanted and—"

He growled.

She cleared her throat. "I've worked hard the last two months to find some stability. By myself."

"You're not alone anymore."

Her lips firmed. "I'm the only person I can trust. I'm going to make sure he or she has everything they need. I... have to depend on me. For my baby."

"*Our* baby." God, he felt a little sick. The poor kid was stuck with him, and he had no idea how to be a father.

"You look green just saying that," she whispered.

"I never wanted kids. I need to...adjust to the idea."

"Well, I need to adjust, too. I've gotten used to being on my own." She rubbed her temple. "It's been a crazy evening, and I'd like to go home and rest."

Bram wanted to argue. He didn't want her out of his sight.

But the look she gave him was pure steel. Addie was tougher than people realized.

With a nod, he rose. "I'll take you home."

"Thank you."

"But Addie—" he waited until she met his gaze "—from now on, you aren't alone, and I'm looking after you. Both of you."

ADDIE TRIED to control her nerves as Bram pulled his big, black Dodge Ram to a stop down the block from her apartment building in Alphabet City.

It wasn't the best building on the street, but the tiny apartment was all she could afford. She was trying to save everything she could for the baby's arrival.

Still, she didn't want Bram to see the place. She knew he hadn't loved her last apartment—he'd complained it wasn't secure enough—and it had been much nicer.

"I can walk from here—"

"I'm seeing you to the door, Addie."

"There's no need. I don't want to put you out."

He ignored her, knifed out of the truck, and circled the hood.

Her gaze snagged on him. She loved the way he moved. He was so big and tall and broad, and she knew that body was solid muscle, but he moved quietly. His red hair was the first thing she'd noticed about him. And he always had stubble on his jaw.

She'd first met him when she'd come back to New York after being rescued. Killian had sent Bram to check on her and ensure her apartment was secure. She'd been fascinated by him. He was solid, steady, and strong. She knew some people found him intimidating. It probably didn't help that he was always grumpy. It hadn't taken her long to learn that scowling was second nature to him.

But he'd never intimidated her.

No, he'd made her feel safe for the first time in her life.

He'd kept dropping by to check on her. She'd make him coffee and they'd talk. Or rather she'd talk and ramble on. Bram wasn't much of a talker, but he'd seemed to like listening to her. She'd started to bake things for him—Irish soda bread, scones, Guinness cake. She'd researched every Irish recipe she could find.

And she'd desperately wanted to kiss him.

For a while, she'd believed he wasn't attracted to her. He rarely touched her.

Then she'd spilled coffee on his shirt and fumbled to blot it with a towel. She'd found herself on her knees in front of him...and she'd watched the instant Bram's control had snapped.

She fought back a shiver at the memory. He'd had her naked and crying out his name seconds later.

Like an idiot, she'd tumbled head over heels in love with Bram O'Donovan.

Until he'd crushed her heart like glass.

Or had he?

Turn it off for now, Addie. She was tired and wrung out. Pregnancy, and all the emotion of seeing Bram, and her other little problem that she tried not to think about, had taken it all out of her.

As Bram opened the door, she scanned the street. No one seemed to be watching them.

She relaxed a little, then Bram grabbed her arm and lifted her out of the vehicle.

She almost moaned from being so close to him. Her heart and her brain were still wary, but her hormone-riddled body wanted to press her face to the bare skin at the base of his throat, and breathe him in.

Be sensible, Addie. You have to protect yourself. She made herself step back.

Addie wasn't sure of her footing with him, and with a precious life depending on her, she couldn't afford to stumble.

She headed toward her building, trying not to notice the dingy paint.

Bram grunted, and she knew that was his way of expressing his unhappiness.

She unlocked the front door and led them into the dimly lit entry. She glanced up and saw a muscle ticking in his tight jaw. The stairs creaked as she headed up them. When she unlocked her apartment door, he gave another unhappy grunt.

"It isn't much, but it's enough for me," she said.

"The lock on the door is shite."

"It's fine." She flicked on the light and tried to keep her smile in place.

Her belly did a sickening turn when she spotted the envelope that had been slipped under her door. She quickly picked it up and stuck it under her arm.

"What's that?" he asked.

"Just mail. A neighbor must've picked it up."

But she already knew what was inside. Bile rose in her throat.

She couldn't let Bram see it.

She didn't want anyone to see it.

The tiny apartment had a brick wall, that she thought added character, and a scarred, mismatched wooden floor. The white paint was...fresh. Okay, fresh-ish. The apartment had a pocket-sized kitchen and bathroom, and her bed took up most of the bedroom. The window had a view of the fire escape and the brick wall of the neighboring building.

Her little stash of baby supplies sat on the floor by the bed. Spying the pretty yellow blanket she'd picked out, covered in tiny toy bears, she wanted to smile. Each week, she saved to buy one new thing for the baby. She had her eye on a sweet, little crib that she wanted to get next.

Bram took it all in, his mouth tight.

"I'm adding you to my health insurance," he said.

"Bram—"

He skewered her with a look. "Whatever you need, I'll get it for you."

She wanted so desperately to believe him, but she hadn't forgotten how it felt to be so alone, sick, and heartbroken.

She'd cried so many tears.

"You don't have to worry." She tried for a smile. "I'm saving money. I have a plan."

He grunted. Then he cupped her cheek, his calloused fingers brushing over her skin.

She closed her eyes. It had shocked her at first, seeing how gentle this big, rugged man could be.

Although, there were times when he hadn't been gentle. He'd been rough and needy in the best possible ways. She felt a clench between her legs.

"If you need me, you call. I'll get Hex to add you to my primary caller list. Your calls will come straight to me."

She met his gaze.

His eyes dropped to her lips, then flicked back up. "Promise me you'll call."

"I promise," she whispered.

"Lock up after you let me out."

She nodded.

He stalked out and she closed the door.

"I'm waiting to hear the lock, Addie," he said through the wood.

She flicked it.

"Goodnight, sunshine."

She heard the heavy tread of his steps, then she sagged against the door and closed her eyes. She wanted to call him back.

No. Be strong. Be independent.

She turned. The apartment seemed so empty now that he was gone.

She sighed, then walked over to the envelope she'd set on the table. She opened it, her hand trembling.

It was like the others, written with cut out letters from a newspaper.

You're mine, Adaline.

You can try to get away, but I'll always find you.

Always.

Soon, we'll be together.

With a small cry, she screwed the letter into a ball and tossed it. It hit the floor and rolled under her tiny table.

She pressed her hands to her cheeks. For weeks, she'd felt someone watching her on the street, at the bar, at the grocery store. She'd thought she'd imagined it.

Then the notes had started.

Someone was out there, watching her.

And they knew where she lived.

Tell Bram, her brain urged her. He was a security expert. This kind of thing was his job.

No. This person just had to be someone playing a practical joke. He'd lose interest and go away eventually.

Besides, she wasn't sure she could trust Bram completely yet, either.

Tears welled and she pressed a palm to her belly.

"I'll protect you, baby. No matter what." She pressed her back to the wall, and slid down to the floor. She'd give her baby everything she'd never had. Love, security, unwavering support. "I promise."

CHAPTER THREE

He hated her apartment.

Bram stepped outside and scowled. It wasn't the worst street, but it was definitely the shittiest building on it. And her apartment was crap. Her last place hadn't been great, but she'd decorated it well—pretty pictures, vases, a soft throw blanket on the couch. It had reflected her.

This new place was plain, bland.

Not Addie at all.

Because she's sick and struggling, you dumbass. Because you got her pregnant.

Bram got that queasy feeling again. He stopped on the sidewalk, resting his hands on his hips.

He had no idea how to be a father. His own was gruff and tough and closed off. Bram was all too aware how much like his father he was.

And he hadn't been much of a son or brother either.

Old, faded pain pricked at him. He breathed through

it. After his mom and Fiona had died, he and his father had fallen farther apart.

Bram wasn't made for relationships or love. He couldn't give much to a baby.

But he was good at fighting, killing, and security. He'd keep Addie and the child safe.

He strode over to his truck, scanning the street out of habit. He slid into the driver's seat, but he didn't start the engine. He wasn't going anywhere.

He couldn't bear the thought of being too far from Addie. He'd stay right here for the night and keep watch.

He slid his hand in his pocket and pulled out a small, wooden carving. It fit in the palm of his hand. It was a ballerina in a tutu, arms raised. *Addie.* The dancer didn't have a face, but the shape of it, the gentle curves of her body, were pure Addie. He'd made it—his secret little hobby that he'd never told anyone about. He'd always been good with his hands.

Turning the tiny statue over, he imagined her smiling.

His phone vibrated and his pulse leaped. Maybe it was Addie? He slipped the carving back into his pocket and pulled out his phone.

"Hellfire" was written on the screen. He shook his head. He was still more than a little bemused by Devyn "Hellfire" Hawke.

His boss' new wife was a little wild, a hell of a CIA agent, fearless, and a whole lot of stubborn. After saving each other's backs on a mission in San Francisco, she'd decided they were new best friends.

Bram didn't have a best friend. He hung out with Nick, Matteo, and Killian from work. They were good guys, even if they couldn't keep up with him when he opened a bottle of good Irish whiskey.

You okay, big guy?

Fine.

If you didn't hear, I just snorted. You can't be okay. You just found your girl and found out you're going to be a dad.

Bram scowled. He hated texting. Still, it was better than actually talking.

I'm fine.

Don't make me come over there.

You don't know where I am.

Bram, I'm a former spy turned new co-owner of Sentinel Security. I can find you.

He sighed.

I can't be a dad. I'll fuck it up.

You don't know that.

My dad isn't that great. I'm not good with people. And I know nothing about babies.

No one knows anything about babies until you have one of your own. Bram, you're protective, and under the

26

gruff, you care. That's all you need. And Addie will help. You're in this together.

> *She thinks I rejected her. I'm not sure she even wants me around. I don't know what to say to her.*

Show her you want her. You don't have to talk. She liked you enough to let you get her pregnant, so I think you'll be fine.

> *I'm not sure that you're the right person to give me relationship advice.*

Hello. I just got married, Bram.

> *After giving Killian the runaround for years.*

Well, we got there in the end. And it's awesome.

When she gave him a string of heart emojis, Bram scowled.

> *Stop.*

Just show her that you're there for her, Bram. See what she likes, what she needs, and give it to her.

Actually, that wasn't bad advice.

> *Okay. Stop bugging me now.*

Love you too, big guy.

Jeez, he was never going to shake Devyn. He looked

out the window, staring blindly at the street. He realized that having Devyn in his life...didn't actually bother him that much.

He turned his phone over in his hand, then flicked open his photos. He found the one he'd looked at a lot over the last few weeks.

Addie.

She was smiling for the camera, her blonde hair spilling everywhere, and only wearing his T-shirt. Her cheeks were flushed, her eyes shining with happiness. He'd just finished making love to her when he'd taken this.

He wanted her like this, all the time. Not pale and tired, with uncertainty and sadness in her eyes.

Give her what she needs.

He could do that.

Starting with a better place to stay, making sure she ate, and not having to be on her feet at a bar for hours on end.

He tapped his fingers on the steering wheel, his thoughts churning, and plans forming. He needed to gain back her trust. He scowled. Why the hell hadn't he gotten her messages?

He shot a message to Hex.

Any idea why I didn't get Addie's messages?

It didn't take her long to respond.

I'm looking into it, Bram. Should have something for you soon.

Thanks. Can you make sure she's added to my caller list?

Already done.

Right. Now what things did a pregnant woman need?

He tapped on his phone and started searching.

He frowned. Information on prenatal vitamins, morning sickness remedies, body pillows and more filled the small screen.

What the hell was a breast pump?

Fuck.

PACING HER TINY APARTMENT, Addie smoothed her hands over her belly.

"We're okay, baby."

She was still confused, her emotions churning. But that wasn't unusual lately. Her hormones had her all over the place. The other day, she'd cried at an ad for coffee on the TV.

She also had a violent craving for cookie dough ice cream with salt-and-vinegar chips. Together. It was weird, but it was what she wanted.

She checked her freezer and found only an empty ice tray.

"Sorry, baby. I'll get some ice cream tomorrow."

She turned, and spied the scrunched-up note on the floor. Her stomach rolled. It had to just be someone playing some sick joke on her.

But who would do that?

It had all started a few weeks after Bram had left.

She'd hoped when she'd moved apartments and jobs that whoever it was would stop.

But they hadn't.

The notes had kept coming.

Fear felt like a rough hand squeezing her insides. She wanted Bram.

No. You're stronger than this. You don't need a man. A hot shower and some sleep were what she needed.

It'd been a big day, and seeing Bram had left her shaken up. She checked her locks and turned the lights off, but left the lamp in the living room on.

She hated the dark. Ever since she was a kid, it had freaked her out. Her mom told her to grow up and quit wasting money. She'd always made Addie turn off the light and sleep, terrified, in the darkness.

Now that Addie was an adult and on her own, she could do what she wanted. When Bram had stayed over, he'd never made her turn the lamp off or made her feel silly about it.

She bit her lip, then grabbed the note off the floor and shoved it in the top drawer in the kitchen with the others. Out of sight, out of mind.

The same couldn't be said for the big Irishman. He was still in her thoughts when she headed for the shower. She turned on the water, then stripped off her On the Rocks uniform. Steam filled the small room, fogging the mirror.

For a second, she was back in her old apartment. A strong memory hit her—rich and vibrant. Her and Bram, naked. He was so much bigger than her. He was crowding in behind her in the bathroom.

Grip the counter, sunshine. His voice was like gravel, that sexy, Irish accent making her belly flutter. His fingers had slid between her thighs, stroking her.

Her moans, the way he'd filled her, taking her from behind.

She closed her eyes, reliving every second. She moaned.

Addie jolted. *Oh, God.* Her body was humming with need, her nipples were hard, and she was wet between her thighs.

Swallowing, she got in the shower. The warm water on her sensitive skin made her moan. She cupped her breasts. They were already larger, and she imagined Bram's rough hands on them.

"*Bram,*" she whispered.

She let one hand drift down, over her round belly, and between her legs.

"Oh." Heat washed over her. She nudged her folds and found her clit. "*Please,* touch me, Bram."

In her mind, she heard his accented voice urging her on, telling her that she was beautiful. That she was his sunshine.

She wanted him here. His hands on her, his big body pressed against hers, his big cock filling her.

Addie came. Her body shook, her moans echoing in the small shower stall.

She stood there, letting the water pulse over her as she came down. Then, the aloneness came. The feeling of being hollow.

She turned off the water, the cool air hitting her skin.

But there was one thing she excelled at, and that was picking herself up and getting on with things.

She wasn't going to slink home to Georgia, a failure. Her mom had already shared her thoughts on Addie's pregnancy.

You're a fool, girl. Your life is ruined. No more dancing for you. It'll be work, a good-for-nothing man, if one will take you on, and more squalling kids. At least your father married me when he knocked me up.

Her baby would be loved and cherished. Her baby would *never* feel like a mistake or a burden. She would always encourage her child to follow their dreams.

Did that mean she should let Bram in?

She bit her lip and toweled off. A part of her wanted to trust him, the part of her that was desperately in love with him.

But maybe she didn't really know him. They'd only spent a week and a half together. Maybe this was lust, not love?

Maybe she was spinning fantasies out of nothing, like her mother always said.

No. She straightened her shoulders. She always tried to think positively. She wasn't going to fall into her mother's defeatist way of thinking.

Addie pulled on some panties, then a large T-shirt that she'd started sleeping in since her pajama shorts had gotten tight around her middle.

The shirt was Bram's.

It was plain white, soft. She fingered it. He'd left it at her place the day before he'd disappeared from her life.

Well, now he's back, and you have to decide how to deal with him.

She wasn't going to let her heart get shattered again in the process. She squeezed some toothpaste on her brush and started cleaning her teeth.

A sound in the living room caught her ear.

She frowned, her hand stilling, and waited.

She couldn't hear anything now, and she shook her head. She quickly finished brushing and rinsed her mouth. She flicked off the light in the bathroom.

There. A scratching sound.

Her heart thumped. Quietly, she headed out to the living area.

The lamp gave off a soft glow.

There was more scratching. Ugh, if it was a mouse, she'd scream. They were cute and all, but she did not want one scampering over her foot or living in her house. She shuddered.

It wasn't a mouse. The scratching was at her front door. Her pulse picked up speed. What was that?

She watched the door handle move.

Now, her heart jumped into her throat and lodged there.

Someone was trying to pick the lock and break in!

Everything inside her went haywire, and she backed up.

Crap. What should she do?

She raced to the table and grabbed her cellphone. Her hands were shaking. She saw Bram's number and stabbed at the screen. She missed and stabbed again.

It rang once.

"Addie?"

His deep voice was a balm that immediately stopped her from falling into a full-blown panic attack. *"Bram,"* she whispered.

"What's wrong?" His tone was deep, and she felt his heightened attention through the phone.

"There's someone at my front door. They're picking the lock—"

She heard him curse. "I'm coming."

"Bram..." She was so afraid.

"Go to the bathroom. Lock yourself in."

She headed that way, licking her dry lips. "Bram, I'm afraid."

"I'm coming, sunshine. Hold on. Now, get in the bathroom."

She scrambled in. The air was still steamy. She locked the door, but she was highly conscious of the flimsy, little, thumb-turn lock.

She wrapped an arm around her belly, and sucked in a shaky breath. She needed a weapon. She had no idea how long it would take Bram to get here.

She opened a drawer and rooted around. She grabbed a can of hair spray and pulled it out.

Then there was a loud crash from her living room.

She gasped, fear flooding her veins.

"Bram! They broke down the front door!"

"Hold on, Addie. I'm coming."

CHAPTER FOUR

Bram sprinted across the street and pressed his phone to his ear.

"Bram?" a deep voice said.

"Wolf, I'm nearly at Addie's. She called me. Someone broke down her front door."

"I'm on my way," Nick "Wolf" Garrick clipped out. "Don't kill anyone."

Bram shoved the phone back in his pocket. He reached the front door of her building, and found it ajar.

He shouldered through.

If the fucker hurt Addie, Bram would kill him.

He thundered up the stairs and saw her door was open.

As he raced inside, he spotted a big guy, wearing a black ski mask. He was banging on the bathroom door. The asshole was as tall as Bram.

Pure, red-hot anger flooded him. He strode across the living room, and gripped the back of the man's black shirt.

The guy jolted. Bram wrenched him backward, and the guy hit Addie's tiny table. It collapsed under the weight of him, wood splintering.

With a growl, the man launched himself at Bram.

A big fist caught Bram's shoulder, and he swallowed a growl. Then he attacked.

He punched the man in the face, chest, gut. This asshole had come after Addie. Had terrified her.

And no doubt had much worse planned.

Energy flooded Bram. He blocked the man's next hit, then shoved the guy. The man hit the wall and Bram elbowed him in the face.

The man cursed, almost too low to hear. It sounded like another language.

"Who the fuck are you?" Bram demanded.

The man didn't respond. He charged at Bram.

They crashed into the couch, and a lamp fell off a side table and smashed. Bram tried to yank the man's mask off.

"You don't breathe Addie's air," Bram said. "You don't come anywhere near her, or I'll kill you. She's mine."

The man's head jerked up. Through the gap in his mask, Bram saw a flare in the man's dark-brown eyes.

He didn't like hearing that.

"Mine," Bram said again.

With a low roar, the attacker jerked his arms up.

He caught Bram in the gut. Bram grunted and blocked the pain, as he'd been trained to do. They hit the floor, wrestling. An elbow hit Bram's already bruised eye, and pain exploded through his face, but he gritted his teeth.

He wasn't letting go.

He had to protect Addie.

"Bram!" Addie's muffled shout. "Are you okay?"

He heard the fear in her voice.

He pinned the attacker down and gripped his shirt. Then Bram hauled him up and punched him in the face.

"I'll always protect her. Always be her shield."

They scuffled again. A hard shove had Bram's shoulder hitting the wall.

Suddenly, the asshole turned and ran.

With a curse, Bram raced to the door. He heard the man hammering down the stairs.

Bram gritted his teeth, his jaw creaking. He wanted to follow. He wanted to catch the fucker and ensure he stayed the hell away from Addie.

But as he looked back into the apartment, he realized he couldn't leave her. She was afraid, and he couldn't leave her alone and unprotected.

He crossed the living room and rapped his knuckles on the bathroom door. "Addie? It's okay. He's—"

The bathroom door wrenched open, and Addie threw herself into his arms with a sob. "I was so scared."

"Shh." He picked her up, the need to soothe her drumming in his chest. He made it to the couch, sat, and settled her on his lap. "You're safe now."

"He's truly gone?"

"Yes." He stroked a hand over her head, and down her back. "He's gone."

"Bram—" Her voice cracked.

He tucked her face to his neck and held her tight. He closed his eyes, relishing the feel of her in his arms. He'd missed her so damn much. So many nights he'd reached for her, and only found empty sheets.

He ran a hand down to her hip. She made a sound and shifted, and he hoped to hell he could keep his cock under control.

Then his fingers brushed her belly. He froze.

She lifted her head. She was fresh-faced, no makeup, and so damn sweet and beautiful. As always, she smelled like spring flowers. He had no right to touch her.

"It's okay." She took his palm and pressed it to her belly. "The baby's about the size of a bell pepper. Although I think our baby might be a little bigger."

He splayed his fingers, his chest tightening. Her stomach was firm, and he couldn't believe that there was a baby in there.

One they'd made together.

"It amazes me every day," she murmured. "I'm going to be the best mom ever."

God, he hoped the baby looked like Addie. He caressed her stomach. She shifted, and he realized she was only wearing a large T-shirt. Most of her impossibly long legs and golden skin were on display.

Then he frowned. "This is my T-shirt."

She tucked a strand of hair behind her ear. "You left it. My pajamas don't fit anymore, so..."

Damn. He liked it. He liked knowing that all this time she'd been wearing something of his. He toyed with the hem and saw her chest hitch. He looked up, and found her cheeks were pink.

"Addie..."

"Bram, I..." She leaned forward and pressed her lips to his.

Yes. Desire exploded like a fist to his gut. It never took much with Addie to leave him hungry. Everything about her entranced him.

He shouldn't be touching her, but his tongue slipped into her mouth, and he cupped the back of her head. He kissed her back.

She made a hungry sound and straddled him. She slid her hands into his hair. "I missed you," she panted. "I missed this."

His heart knocked against his ribs. He slid his other hand down and cupped her ass over her panties.

She moaned, grinding down on his erection, which was now as hard as steel.

"Sunshine." The word ended on a rough groan. He wanted to lay her on the couch and strip her naked. He wanted his face between her thighs.

There was pure need on her face. *"Bram."*

Then the sound of a clearing throat abruptly interrupted them. "Everyone's okay, I see."

Addie squeaked, and Bram's hands tightened on her. He glanced over her shoulder at the door.

Nick Garrick's muscular form filled the doorway, and the man was fighting a smile. But as Bram's friend took in the upturned living area, his smile faded.

Bram spun Addie back around on his lap. "The attacker fled. He was wearing a ski mask. Big guy. Didn't say anything."

Addie blinked, and for the first time noticed the mess in her living room. "Oh my God. My table."

"And the guy clocked you, I see," Nick said.

"I hit him harder."

"Bram." Distraught, Addie touched the swelling at the corner of his eye.

"It's fine." He'd put ice on it later. He looked back at Nick. "Get Hex to pull any CCTV. He was big, about my height, black mask, black clothes, brown eyes."

Nick grunted and straightened a chair. "Addie, has anyone been bothering you? At work? A customer, maybe?"

"Oh." Her gaze skittered away. "Let me think. I mean, something like that would be obvious."

Bram tensed. Addie tended to ramble when she was fudging the truth.

"No." She shook her head and refused to look at either of them. "I can't think of anyone."

She was lying. He gripped her chin and made her look at him. "Sunshine, I'm going to keep you safe. But to do that, we need to find the man responsible."

She nodded. "Maybe he was just a random thief?"

"He was after you. He was trying to get to you."

Her hands tightened on his shirt. "Bram..."

"I'm here." He stroked his fingers along her jaw. "Tell us what you know."

She bit her lip. "Promise you won't lose it?"

Bram scowled.

She tossed a frantic look at Nick. "Please. I don't want Bram hurt."

Nick straightened. "Bram's a tough guy, Addie, and

the most levelheaded guy I know. Whatever you know, you need to share it, so we can help."

She nodded, then pointed to the kitchen. "Top drawer."

Nick opened the drawer and pulled out a crumpled piece of paper then another and another. As Nick looked at them, Bram saw his friend's face harden.

He looked up. "Bram, you'd better take a look at these."

AS BRAM SET Addie on the couch, he squeezed her shoulder, and she savored his strong touch. That quiet show of support.

But as he walked over to join Nick, butterflies—nervous ones—took flight in her belly.

She clenched her hands together and watched as he read the first note, then the next. His face hardened to granite. It was like watching a storm cloud forming.

He muttered a curse.

"Keep a lock on it," Nick said quietly.

Bram's head jerked up. God, the look on his face.

"How long have you been getting these?" Bram bit out.

She swallowed. "A few months. Just after...you left."

He looked at the notes again. With a growl, he scrunched them up in one fist.

"Hey, we could get something off those." Nick took them back. He opened a few more drawers before finding a Ziploc bag to slide them into.

Bram strode back to Addie, his big body tense. He dropped down beside her on the couch. "What else? Has it just been notes?"

She sucked in a breath. "Sometimes I feel like someone is watching me on the street, at the store—"

He cursed.

She gripped her hands together. "I thought I was imagining it."

"You didn't imagine those notes." His voice was gruff.

She bit her lip. "I hoped they were a prank or a bad joke."

"Until someone busted your door down," he growled.

Emotions swung around inside her and tears welled in her eyes.

"Don't cry."

She sniffed. "Ordering someone not to cry doesn't work, Bram. Especially if they're pregnant."

"I...hate tears."

"I can't help it."

Bram's scowl deepened, then he yanked her to his chest.

She clung to him. "I didn't know what to do. At the time, I was confused and worried, and I'd just found out I was pregnant." She paused. "I couldn't contact you, and then I needed to find a new job and apartment."

He ran a hand down her spine. "It's okay, Addie. It's going to be okay. I'm going to find this piece of shit and keep you safe."

She pulled in a shuddering breath.

"I'll take the notes into the office," Nick said. "I'll let

Hex take a look at them and check CCTV. It's not safe for Addie to stay here."

"I know." Bram smoothed her hair back from her face. "Pack a bag, sunshine. You're coming with me."

She blinked. "What?"

"You're moving in with me. My place at the Sentinel Security warehouse is secure."

And Bram would be there.

He touched her stomach gently, a little less panic in his eyes this time. "And you have the baby to protect, too."

She pressed a hand over his. The baby was the most important thing in her world.

"I can keep you both safe at Sentinel Security," he said.

She nodded. "Let me change and pack some things."

Relief crossed his rugged face before his features fell back into their normal, stoic look. "Good. Go on, I'll finish talking with Nick."

Addie hurried out, skirting her destroyed table. Her stomach clenched. The man had come here to hurt her.

What if Bram hadn't been close?

What if Bram had been hurt in the fight?

She stroked her belly. "It's okay, baby. Your daddy is going to keep us safe."

Soon, Addie had changed into black leggings, ballet flats, and her favorite pink sweater. She packed a small suitcase. She spotted her well-worn pointe shoes resting on a shelf, and touched them. She wasn't sure she'd ever dance again. She loved it, but she'd never adjusted to the grind of endless auditions and rejections. To never quite having enough money to cover the rent and bills.

The dream hadn't been what she'd imagined.

She heard the low rumble of Bram and Nick's voices in her kitchen. When she stepped out of the bedroom, Bram hurried over to take her small suitcase.

"Nick will stay and secure your front door."

"Thanks, Nick," she murmured.

The bearded man nodded. "Sure thing, sweetheart. Get some rest."

Bram took her hand. When they reached the door, and she saw the broken frame, a shiver rocked through her.

He wrapped his arm around her shoulders and led her down the stairs. Before she knew it, he had her bundled into his truck. Nervously, she looked around the street.

Was her attacker still out there? Was he watching them?

Bram reached over and squeezed her arm. "I'm not letting anyone get you."

She nodded. "Thanks, Bram."

He grunted. "You don't have to thank me. Let's get you safe so you can get some sleep."

At this time of night, the drive to the Sentinel Security warehouse in Chelsea wasn't too long. Soon, Bram pulled his big truck into an underground parking lot beneath the warehouse.

After a short elevator ride, they stepped into a long corridor. She took in the arched windows at the end of the hall, and the polished-concrete floor.

Bram used a fancy palm scanner lock to open his front door. "This is my place."

She walked in and her mouth dropped open.

The apartment was huge and modern. She imagined it was filled with light during the day. It had a concrete floor, and touches of wood and gray. It was very masculine. Very Bram. There were some bookcases against one wall, but not much on them. A couple of large, tan-leather couches sat in front of a huge television screen.

If this was her place, she'd add some color. Some pictures, maybe a plant or two. And books. She'd fill the shelves with books.

"Here." He led her down the hallway. "You must be tired."

The bedroom was large, with a huge bed with a wooden headboard. It was covered in dark-green covers. There were more arched windows that let in the glint of city lights. A large mirror leaned against one wall, and there was a wooden dresser.

"This is your room," she said.

"Yeah. I'll sleep on the couch. I don't have a bed in the other bedroom." He shrugged a shoulder. "I don't have guests."

She hoped that meant women, too. She bit her lip. "Thanks again, Bram. For saving me."

"Always." He shifted, and looked like he wanted to touch her. "You're safe now. Get some sleep."

He strode over to the bathroom and flicked on the light. "I know you like some light. I'll leave this on for you."

Her heart thumped. "Thanks."

"Good night, Addie."

After he'd left, Addie sat on the edge of the bed. It was so big she was sure she would get lost in it. She sighed. She was pretty tired, and the adrenaline had left her system, leaving her even more exhausted.

She splashed her face with water in the very cool bathroom, decorated with gray tiles and green towels. Bram's bathroom. She glanced at the huge shower. He showered in there. Instantly, her brain painted the image of his big body, naked and wet.

She knew exactly how his muscled body looked, the light smattering of hair on his chest.

There was a tug low in her belly.

Damn. Someone had attacked her and here she was, drooling over Bram. She was blaming the pregnancy hormones.

She found a simple, white nightgown in her suitcase, that, while short, still fit over her belly. Just.

When she got into the bed, she moaned. The sheets smelled like Bram. That leather and spice scent that was embedded in her senses. She pressed her face into the pillow, and breathed deeply.

Finally, she felt safe. The tension of the last few hours, days, and weeks was beginning to drain away.

Safe.

She cradled her belly.

For now, she could let go of the worry, stress, and fear. She knew with absolute certainty that Bram was out there, and would stop anything or anyone who came through the door. He'd already fought for her tonight.

Because you're pregnant and he feels responsible, a voice in her head whispered. *Not because he wants you.*

Addie banged her fist against the pillow. She wasn't sure how she felt.

Did she want Bram to want her? The truth was, she was still in love with him. She wanted him, but not because he felt she was a chore, or a burden.

It took a while, but she finally drifted off to sleep, Bram's scent in her senses. She must have dreamed, because she was certain she felt a rough hand stroke her hair, and an accented voice whisper, "I'll keep you safe, I promise."

CHAPTER FIVE

The next morning, Bram quietly opened the front door to his apartment and slipped inside.

He'd woken up early after an uncomfortable night on the couch. He'd stewed over this fucker stalking Addie.

Maybe it was some sick fuck who'd seen her dance?

Mine. The word echoed in his head. He wasn't letting *anyone* near her.

He carried the shopping bags in his hands into the kitchen. He fucking hated shopping.

He paused to listen. The apartment was still as quiet as it had been when he'd left this morning, and Addie had been fast asleep. His muscles clenched. When he'd checked on her, she'd been curled around a pillow in the center of his bed. He'd had to fight not to touch her.

She needed her sleep.

He'd left her a note, but it was still untouched on the island in the kitchen.

He dropped the bags on the floor beside the island,

and started the coffee machine. Only moments later, he heard the quiet pad of bare feet.

He turned and his throat closed.

Addie's sunny blonde hair was a wild, tangled mess, her legs were bare and golden. She wore a tiny scrap of white that pulled tight over her belly.

"Bram." She rubbed her eyes, still sleepy.

"Morning. Did you sleep all right?"

"Like a rock. It was the best sleep I've had in..." she tilted her head. "A really long time."

"Coffee?" He pulled a mug out of the cupboard.

"No, thanks." She touched her belly. "I'm off caffeine. Do you have any juice?"

"Yeah. Sit down."

She slid onto a stool at the island. "I need to call Paddy today and talk about my shifts."

Bram frowned. "You can't work at the bar."

She blinked. "Bram, I need to work. I need the paycheck."

"I'll take care of you."

She straightened. "I can take care of myself."

He poured her some orange juice. "Never said you couldn't, but you aren't alone anymore. I'll take care of you and the baby. It isn't safe for you in the bar while someone is after you. You'd be putting yourself, the staff, and the bargoers at risk."

"Oh." Her face fell, and she rubbed her belly. "I don't want anyone to get hurt."

So damn caring. "Then talk to Paddy today."

She nodded.

When Bram brought her juice over to her, he nudged a shopping bag toward her with his foot.

"What's all of this?" she asked.

"It's for you."

She blinked. "Me?"

He hauled the bags onto the island. "Stuff expectant mothers need."

Addie just looked at him. "How do you know what expectant mothers need?"

He cleared his throat. "I Googled it." And sent Hex a message. Or seven. He was pretty sure the tech guru had been laughing at his questions.

Addie reached into the closest bag and pulled out a maternity nightgown and matching robe in soft-blue stripes.

"Oh." She stroked the fabric.

"If you want more of my T-shirts, I have plenty."

"This is so pretty." She pulled a long pillow out next.

"Lady at the store said it's good for sleeping, for pregnant women." He felt heat creep up the back of his neck.

Addie pulled out a blanket next. It was really soft, and a pretty, pink color. She stroked it.

"Um, I know you had a similar one at your place. There are some things for the bath. And other...stuff. Anything you don't want, I'll return."

"Bram..." Her voice was breathy.

When he saw tears in her eyes, panic swooped in. *Shit.* "If you hate it all—"

"*No.*" She grabbed his hand. "I love it. I... No one's done anything like this for me."

He made a low sound and stepped closer, wrapping his arms around her.

She held on tight and pressed her face to his chest. They didn't talk, and he just stroked her back. He didn't really know what to say, but he just wanted those tears to go away.

When she finally tipped her face up, he saw the tears were gone, and there was simmering heat in their place.

Feck. He tried to find some control. She was pregnant, vulnerable, and still rumpled from sleep.

"Bram?"

He grunted.

"Please..." She hesitated.

"I'll give you whatever you need, Addie." He was so weak.

"Please kiss me."

He couldn't deny her. He lowered his head.

She tasted like orange juice and sunshine. He groaned, and parted her lips, slipping his tongue into her mouth.

She made a husky sound and slid her arms around his neck.

Sensation rushed through him. Desire mixed with the unbelievable feeling that this sweet, beautiful woman wanted him.

Bram slid his tongue against hers, wanting more, wanting to imprint himself on her.

She gripped his arms, pressing into his body. "Bram, I need you."

He deepened the kiss, desire pumping through him.

He'd give her everything she wanted. He went to lift her off the stool when his cellphone rang.

He swallowed a curse. "That's Hex's ring tone."

Addie smoothed her hands down his shirt. "It might be important."

"Yes." Reluctantly, he stepped back, conscious of the erection pressing against his zipper. He pulled his phone out. "Hex."

"Bram, command center, now." Her usual teasing tone was missing.

"What did you find?" he asked.

"Something that pisses me off. Bring Addie. Tell her I've got some muffins and a smoothie for her and the bump."

"We're on our way." He ended the call. "Hex has some information for us."

"On my stalker?"

"I'm not sure." He helped her down, then tried not to touch her as she hurried off to get changed.

When they walked into the office, he still really, really wanted to touch her. He let himself press a hand to her lower back.

Screens on the desks in Hex's area were filled with information, as was the large, interactive screen that covered one wall.

"There you are." Hex bounded up from her chair.

She often reminded Bram of a toy that never ran out of batteries.

"Addie, I have a blueberry muffin and fruit smoothie for you. Lots of fruit is good for the mini Bram."

Shit. He barely controlled his jolt. A mini him? No. He couldn't picture it.

Addie accepted the drink and the muffin with a smile. "Thanks, Hex. I'm getting spoiled this morning."

"Oh?" Hex cocked an eyebrow and sat there grinning. "Did Bram get you something better? Breakfast in bed? A morning orgasm?"

Addie choked on the smoothie, then laughed, her cheeks turning pink. "No. Expectant-mom things."

"Ah, now I get all the text messages I was bombarded with." Hex's grin dissolved. "I have some news for you." She skewered Bram with a look. "Now, don't lose your shit."

Addie looked worried, and Bram pressed a hand to her shoulder. "Tell us."

"I managed to track down the messages Addie left you, Bram."

He frowned. "Why didn't I get them?"

"Someone made sure you didn't."

"Someone hacked our system?" He couldn't believe that. Hex was a fiend when it came to cybersecurity.

"No." Anger crossed her face. "It was someone on the inside."

"What?" That made no sense. Someone from Sentinel Security had stopped Addie getting in touch with him.

"It was the same someone who Addie spoke with upstairs when she visited."

"Tell me," he demanded.

Addie gasped. "The woman in reception."

Hex nodded and cleared her throat. "Pam."

Bram frowned. "Who?"

"God, men are so clueless. Pam. She works in reception. She has a massive crush on you."

His frown deepened as he thought. "Brunette? Late thirties?"

"That's her," Hex said. "Divorced, and an experienced office receptionist who's good at her job. Except when a young, beautiful blonde keeps trying to get in touch with the hot, gruff guy she has her eye on."

Anger welled inside Bram. It was small at first, but swelled. Because this woman he barely knew was petty, Addie had gone through hell, and thought he'd abandoned her. It had left her in danger. He growled.

Hex's bi-colored eyes popped open in alarm. "Bram—"

"She in?"

"Bram, listen—"

"Hex, is she in?"

"Yes."

He swiveled and headed for the door.

ADDIE RACED AFTER BRAM.

She shot a panicked look at Hex, who was keeping pace beside her. The other woman pulled a face.

Bram looked like a thundercloud. Addie felt the crackle of electricity coming from him.

The three of them slid into the elevator, and Bram stabbed at a button.

"Bram—" Hex started.

"No," he growled. "That woman stepped out of line. Addie was trying to reach me, with important information, and this woman, for her own fucked-up reasons, blocked the messages."

"I get it. And I'll be telling Killian. Pam will be gone before the end of the day. I've already sent him a message."

Addie wrung her hands together. She couldn't believe a woman would be this petty.

She tried to be understanding, but she really didn't like the fact that this woman had a thing for Bram, and she'd caused Addie a lot of heartache.

"She'll still be getting a piece of my mind." Bram's hands balled into fists.

He wasn't a storm, he was a big, grumpy bomb about to detonate.

Without thinking, Addie stepped close to him. "Bram, just take a breath. Everything worked out."

He gripped her hips, and, startled, she pressed her hands to his chest.

"Her lies made you think I'd abandoned you. You were alone, looking for a new job and apartment."

"I know," she whispered. "But I made it."

He made an annoyed sound. "Your apartment is shit, and you were on your feet in a bar, pregnant. And now... Now I learn you've been in danger for months. Some asshole is stalking you, and I didn't know because of this woman." He pulled Addie up on her toes and slid a hand into her hair.

Her heart was pounding; his cologne surrounded her. "Bram—"

"He could've hurt you." His eyes boiled with emotion. "And that woman is to blame, and so is my own fucked-up stupidity in not asking Hex to find you sooner."

Addie's heart flip-flopped. He wasn't just angry at this Pam woman, he was angry at himself.

She went up on her toes and brushed her lips along his jaw. "It's not your fault. We found each other, and you saved me. We'll work it out."

He pulled her closer, breathed her in. She sensed some of the terrible tension drain out of him, but not all of it.

The elevator doors opened.

He let her go, but took her hand.

Addie glanced at Hex, and the woman winked at her. As Bram towed her out, she heard Hex whisper. "You tamed the beast."

He pulled her through a hall of offices, then into the main reception area of Sentinel Security.

She'd been here before, but it had all been a blur. Now she took in the plush reception done in cool blues with modern furniture, and the Sentinel Security logo etched on the wall—a gold shield with a stylized S in the center.

Two neat and tidy receptionists sat at a high desk, and when the older of the two rose from her chair, butterflies went crazy in Addie's belly.

Pam was neat and professional, her brown hair well cut, but seeing her, knowing what she'd done, made one butterfly leap up and lodge in Addie's throat.

"Pam," Bram rumbled.

She shot him a dazzling smile. "Bram." She skirted the desk. She wore a skirt suit in a rich blue. "How are you?"

"Pissed."

Pam froze, and her gaze flicked to Addie and her mouth flattened. Then she looked at Addie's stomach, and her face turned a sickly color. "I'm so—"

"Quiet. I just found out Addie left me messages that were *deliberately* not forwarded to me."

Pam clutched her hands together.

"And she came here to see me, and was turned away. By you."

The older woman swallowed. "Bram—"

"By a rude, deluded, petty woman," he added.

Pam jerked.

"Addie is mine. She's pregnant with my baby, and she was scared and alone, and you lied to her."

"I... I..."

He leaned forward. "You left her in danger. You left my baby in danger."

Pam's lips flattened. "I'm sorry," she whispered. "I didn't know."

"You should be sorry," he growled.

"Bram." Addie pressed into his side and slid her hand across his hard, flat stomach. She was feeling a little sorry for Pam, despite everything.

The other woman's gaze fell to where Addie touched him, and her face twisted.

Okay, maybe Addie didn't feel that sorry.

She let herself remember the fear, the worry, the

terrible ache when she'd been alone and thought Bram had abandoned her. She glared at the woman.

Pam lifted her chin. "I like you, Bram. I thought if you gave me a chance, we'd be good together." She sniffed. "Then I realized you're like all the other men out there. You wanted a blonde schoolgirl."

Addie rolled her eyes. "I'm twenty-six years old."

"Give it a few more years, and he'll trade you in for a younger model," Pam said. "They all do."

"Be quiet," Bram snapped. "I didn't even know who you were. I've never shown any interest in you."

Pam flinched.

He pressed a hand over Addie's stomach, and she jolted. She loved his hands on her.

Pam followed the movement and her face paled even more.

"She is pregnant with my baby, and you blocked her."

"I didn't know," the other woman said.

"It doesn't matter." Bram's jaw locked tight. "You didn't do your job."

Addie leaned into him even more.

Hex stepped forward. "I've already informed Killian of this breach of protocol."

Now, the last drop of color left Pam's face. "I said I'm sorry. I—"

"It won't be enough to save your job," Hex said. "Pack up your things. Someone from HR will be down to see you soon."

The woman's shoulders dropped.

Bram turned and headed back toward the elevator, keeping Addie's hand tight in his.

"Bram?" She tried to gauge his mood.

Suddenly, he stopped and gently pushed her against the wall. She gasped.

He cupped her face and kissed her.

She still felt the anger simmering inside him, but she melted against him. It was clear that he hated what she'd gone through, and that warmed her heart.

Then he opened his mouth and really kissed her, and Addie forgot all about Pam.

She stroked her tongue against his. He groaned against her lips and slid a big, thick thigh between her legs.

Oh, God. The butterflies in her belly went haywire now. Each lick, nibble, and suck made her body heat rise. Her skin felt hot, and she was close to panting.

Then he pulled back. Ruddy color filled his face.

He ran his hands down her arms. Her belly filled with hot desire, and she wanted him to scoop her up and take her upstairs to that big bed of his.

"Come on, I'm taking you out," he said.

She blinked. "Out?"

"To lunch. I'll make sure we aren't followed."

"Lunch?"

His lips quirked. "On a date." One hand skated along the side of her face. "We never got a chance to do that before. I want to take you somewhere nice."

Her heart did a little pitty-pat. "A date."

He nodded. "Get changed and we'll go."

CHAPTER SIX

B ram drove down the street, battling the traffic. He hated New York's crowded streets. Sometimes he missed the narrow, mostly empty Irish country roads.

He glanced at Addie in the passenger seat of his truck. She was looking out the window, a faint smile on her face. She was glowing. Her skin was luminous.

His hands clenched on the steering wheel in an effort to stop from reaching out and touching her.

He'd given her his phone so she could call Paddy. Her boss had given her time off, told her to stay safe, and to call him if she needed anything. Bram knew he shouldn't feel jealous of the man, but it was clear Addie liked the older bar owner.

Bram forced his hands to relax on the wheel. She wouldn't need Paddy Ryan, because Bram would ensure she had everything she needed.

Thoughts of Pam made him scowl. He was still angry at what the woman had done. Interfering in his life for her own selfish purposes.

"Bram?"

He glanced at Addie. There was worry in her eyes.

"You've got that thundercloud look. If you don't want to go out for lunch—"

"I do. I know a place. It's small, quiet."

And Matteo "Hades" Mancini had gone ahead to scout it out and ensure it was safe. Bram had sent the man strict instructions. He wanted to take her out on a date.

He'd never taken her anywhere. For those ten nights, he'd been crazy for her. They'd mostly eaten take out at her place, but most of the time they'd rarely left her bed. He'd been so hungry for her, and for the way she'd come alive under his hands.

Remembering, his cock tightened. Most of the time, he'd barely made it through the door before he was tearing her clothes off.

Then, he'd gone away on a mission and lost her. He hated that she'd believed that he'd just used her for sex, then left her.

Bram was going to spoil her, treat her the way she deserved to be treated. He'd never spoiled anyone before, but he was going to damn well try.

His phone rang and he touched the dash. "O'Donovan."

"Bram, sorry to interrupt," Killian said. "I wanted to let you know that Pam is gone. Her employment has been terminated immediately." The man's voice was as sharp as a blade.

"Thanks, Killian."

"She made some very bad choices." There was a

pause. "I've managed to hold back my wife from punishing Pam." There was faint amusement in his voice.

Bram's lips twitched. He could only imagine what Devyn had planned.

"Now, Hex said you're taking Addie out to lunch, and I'm sorry to interrupt..."

"What's up?"

Killian sighed. "I got a call from Eamon Farley."

Bram fought the urge to roll his eyes. Farley was an eccentric Irish millionaire who had his fingers in lots of businesses in New York, and owned a lot of artwork. He had a warehouse in the Meatpacking District that he'd converted into a private gallery. Most of the art inside looked like shite to Bram, but Farley gushed over it, and it was worth a small fortune.

Sentinel Security had installed the security system, and Farley had insisted on only dealing with Bram. Irishman to Irishman. He'd said he'd only trust a fellow countryman with his most prized possessions. Bram hadn't minded the work, and liked the wiry, old man.

While Bram was overseeing the installation, Farley would often turn up at the end of the day with a bottle of Teeling 30-year-old single malt whiskey. One of Bram's favorites, and normally out of his price range.

"Farley called, and there's some problem at his gallery," Killian said. "A sensor on one of the displays is malfunctioning and setting an alarm off, but the gallery's empty. He wants it checked out now. And he wants you."

Bram let out a sigh. "It's fine, Killian. I'll swing past and check it out."

"Thanks. I'll see you later. I want an update on

Addie's stalker situation." Killian paused. "And I'll need to update my sister, as well."

Addie gasped. "Um, Killian, I...never mentioned the notes to Saskia."

Killian made a sound.

"Or the baby," Addie continued. "She knew Bram and I...that I thought things hadn't worked out."

"I guessed as much, since on our recent trip to San Francisco my lovely sister skewered Bram with some death glares."

Addie blinked. "Oh, no."

"She'll want to know, Addie," Killian continued. "And that you and Bram have sorted things out."

"Okay."

"Now, go and let Bram deal with this problem for our pesky client, then enjoy your lunch."

"Bye, Killian." Bram ended the call, then turned the truck at the next lights and headed for the Meatpacking District. "Sorry about the delay for lunch."

She smiled. "It's fine, Bram. Actually, I'm excited to see you work."

He grunted. "A lot of my work is boring. Surveillance, making phone calls, installing security systems."

"It's not boring to me."

He felt something in his chest swell. But he reminded himself this wasn't about him. It was about taking care of her.

He couldn't fail her again.

Finally, he pulled up in front of Farley's warehouse, and parked. Addie looked at the whitewashed building and plate-glass windows. There was a sculpture in one window. It looked like a kid had thrown a bunch of colorful play dough together in a pile taller than Addie. The bright yellows, blues, reds, and greens were garish.

"Oh, that's...interesting," she said.

"Farley leans heavily toward *contemporary* art," Bram told her.

She smiled. "You don't like contemporary art?"

He smiled back. "Not my thing."

He preferred art that looked like the thing it was supposed to be.

Her gaze dropped to his mouth and his gut locked. "Addie?"

"Sorry." She cleared her throat.

"Let's sort out the security system and get to lunch," he said.

"For our date."

He took her hand. It was so small and feminine in his. "Yeah, our date."

He used the code to unlock the security system and enter the warehouse.

"This place is only open to the public a few days a week." He frowned at the security panel and noted the blinking light. There was a problem with the pressure sensor in the main room. He saw someone had been in earlier and had armed the system when they'd left. Farley must've come to check it.

Bram and Addie's footsteps echoed in the cavernous building.

"Wow." She glanced around, taking in the pieces of art dotted around the space.

Most of them were wild and colorful paintings, or sculptures that looked like twisted, tortured beings.

"You did the security system for the entire place?" she asked.

"Yes. The art's worth a lot of money. And Farley is a little eccentric. He only wanted me to oversee things, since I was Irish." Bram strode toward the platform in the center. A sculpture that looked like a large poodle made of bottle caps rested on it.

He frowned. It looked like junk to him, but what the hell did he know?

He circled the platform, then stepped up on it.

That's when he heard a distinctive click. It sent a shiver down his spine. It was a click he'd heard before, in war zones. He froze.

Addie took a step closer. "Bram?"

"Don't come any closer." His heart raced. He needed to get her out of here, but he needed her safe.

Carefully, he took out his cellphone, unlocked it, and tossed it toward her. It hit the floor near her feet.

"Addie, take my phone, then get back to the lobby. Call Killian."

"Bram, you're scaring me."

A thought hit him. "Don't leave the building." This could be a ploy by her stalker to snatch her.

She picked up the phone. "What's going on?"

"Just go."

She straightened. "No. I might not be some badass security person, but tell me what's going on so I can help."

Her tone was firm. She wasn't going to let it go.

"I think I just stepped on a bomb."

AFTER GETTING off the phone with Killian, Addie stared at Bram, her belly churning and her pulse racing.

"Addie, get to the lobby," he ordered.

"I'm not leaving you." She licked her dry lips. "Killian is on the way, and he said not to move."

"I'm not going anywhere. I've no idea what we're dealing with, and I want you out of the blast radius."

Blast radius. *God.* She pressed a hand to her belly and backed up a little, but not all the way to the lobby.

"Just stay still," she said. "Killian will get you out."

God, was it really a bomb? If it went off—

A stabbing pain pinched her chest. She couldn't lose him. She'd just gotten him back.

"Addie? Addie?"

She jerked her head up and looked at him across the space.

"Breathe. It's going to be okay."

"What if it's not? I don't want you hurt." Or worse. Her throat was so tight. "I'm never lucky. Anytime things look up, life likes to prove that she's the boss." Her emotions whirled, out of control. "Saskia got me an audition, and I finally got to dance in a great show, then...poof, it's gone."

"You were wonderful in that show."

She jerked. "You saw me?"

He nodded. "I went to see you." He paused. "A few times."

She tried to compute the idea of Bram—big, tough, rugged Bram—going to watch her dance.

"You never told me."

He cleared his throat. "You're a great dancer, Addie. Beautiful. If you want to dance again after the baby comes, you can, and should."

Now she felt a burn in her chest.

"Whatever you want to do, I'll support you," he continued.

First, she needed him safe. Tears welled up, swamping her. Damn her hormones. "*Bram.*" He couldn't miss the fear cracking her voice.

"It's going to be all right, Addie. I promise you."

There was the sound of a door opening and she tensed.

A second later, Killian and Devyn strode in, Hex and a handsome, dark-haired man in a suit were with them.

"Bram, talk to me." Killian looked so cool, composed.

As the others circled the platform, Hex came to Addie and wrapped an arm around her.

"It's going to be fine," the hacker said.

"He's standing on a *bomb*, Hex."

The other woman squeezed her. "He's been in tighter spots."

Addie glanced askance at the woman.

Hex pulled a face. "Sorry, that wasn't helpful, was it?"

Killian lay down on his stomach on the floor, carefully removing the side of the platform. Devyn and the handsome man knelt beside him.

"Fuck. I see it. IED." Killian carefully shifted back,

then rose smoothly to his feet. "Hang tight, Bram. Santi is on the way."

"Who's Santi?" Addie asked.

"Our bomb disposal guy," Hex told her. "Ex-Army. He's the best. Nick's gone to get him."

Time ticked by slowly. It was agonizing watching Bram standing there, knowing he was on a bomb.

"Hadley is going to be pissed she isn't here," Hex said.

"Hadley?"

"The other member of our team. Hadley Lockwood, although she'll be Hadley Knightley before too long. She's engaged to Bennett Knightley."

Addie tried to focus. "The British billionaire?"

"Yes. He's totally gorgeous. Hadley's British too, and they are perfect together." Hex sighed. "Anyway, she's out of town on a job for a few days."

The handsome man strolled over to her and Hex. If Addie wasn't so panicked, she'd probably get tongue-tied at how handsome he was. His dark hair had a hint of a curl, and his smile was very white against his bronze skin.

"He'll be fine. Santi will have the bomb defused in the blink of an eye." He reached out and squeezed Addie's hand. "I'm Matteo. I work with Bram. Why don't you come with us, *cara*? We'll find you a seat."

"I'm not leaving him."

"He wants you safe."

She looked at Matteo's gorgeous face. "I'm *not* leaving."

"All right." She thought she saw a glint of admiration in his dark eyes. "You remind me of my Gabbi. She's soft and sweet on the outside, but pure steel on the inside. I'll bring you a chair. Maybe a little farther back, just to calm *mio amico.*"

Addie nodded.

She'd just sat down when a short man shouldered into the warehouse with Nick.

The man looked to be in his mid-fifties, with salt-and-pepper, curly hair, and was missing one eye. He had terrible, old burn scars down one side of his face. He carried a heavy-duty toolbox in one hand.

"That's Santi. Santi Guzman," Hex said. "A bomb got him, but only because he was ambushed. This man knows bombs inside and out."

"Santi." Killian shook the man's hand. "Bram's on an IED with a pressure sensor. It was part of the security system, but someone tampered with it, and attached it to an explosive."

Santi nodded and opened his toolbox. "Let's take a look."

Addie bit her lip and watched, her nerves strung tight.

The bomb expert got down on his stomach, reaching under the platform.

She twisted her hands together over her belly. Over their baby.

Hex rubbed her back. "Deep breaths. Santi is the best."

The bomb man grunted. "Don't move, *amigo.*"

"I'm not moving," Bram growled.

Santi muttered a few times. "Simple design, nothing fancy."

"Get it defused, Santi," Killian said.

"You'll owe me, Hawke."

Killian snorted. "I pay you a large retainer, from memory."

"A nice bottle of the Fuenteseca Reserva 21-Year-Old tequila should do it."

Bram made a sound. "You need a good bottle of Irish whiskey."

Addie blinked. "They're joking around? Right now?"

Hex squeezed her arm. "It doesn't mean they're not taking it seriously. They're just blowing off steam."

"I can't lose him." Her hand splayed over her stomach. "We can't lose him."

"You're not going to, Addie." Hex crouched in front of her, her face serious. "Bram is tough. Too tough to get hurt. He's been brooding for months, worried about you. He asked me to find you, and now he has you back, and he isn't going anywhere."

Addie swallowed and nodded.

She looked over, and saw Bram was looking at her. Their gazes locked.

Suddenly, Santi sat back.

"It's done. You're all good, Excalibur. If anyone's feeling nervous, they should step back."

No one moved.

Addie sucked in a breath.

Bram stepped off the platform gingerly, and when nothing happened, everyone relaxed. He bent over and put his hands on his knees, sucking in a few breaths.

Devyn slapped his arm. "Nice to see you didn't blow up, bestie."

Bram shot her a look, then turned and strode across the space to Addie.

Relief made her giddy. When he wrapped his arms around her, she leaped into his arms with a small cry. She pressed her lips to his.

He let out a low groan, then opened his mouth and kissed her. When they finally broke apart, he pressed his face to her hair.

"Feck, I was afraid," he whispered.

She clung to him. "You didn't look it."

"I wasn't afraid for myself. I was afraid to leave you... and the baby." He nuzzled her. "I need to hold you tight. Just a bit longer."

"Don't let go." She reveled in the solid feel of him, and the reassuring beat of his heart.

"Hades, find Farley," Killian said sharply. "Find out what the fuck he knows. Bram was lured here."

Addie sucked in a breath. Bram was targeted?

"I'm on it, boss." Matteo headed out with a loose-hipped stride. "Keep your girl safe, Bram."

Bram nodded, then set her down.

"Let's get back to the office," Killian said. "I want to know who the fuck is behind this. No one messes with my clients or my people."

Addie fought back a shiver. She never, ever wanted to be on Killian's bad side.

Bram wrapped an arm around Addie, and she leaned into him.

"It's going to be all right, Addie. I promise."

CHAPTER SEVEN

It wasn't until he walked Addie into the Sentinel Security office that Bram breathed a sigh of relief.

She was safe.

Standing there, knowing a bomb was under him... He'd been sweating, terrified. For Addie.

He didn't care about himself, but he needed to be there for her, and the baby. He pressed his lips together. Who the hell had done this? Had Bram been the target, or was it just some sort of twisted plot to get to Addie?

Who the hell was her stalker, and how far was this asshole willing to go to get her?

"Sit." He found a chair and nudged her into it.

She pulled a face. "You can ask me, Bram. You don't need to manhandle me around."

He scowled. "You know I'm not much of a talker."

She laughed. God, he loved that sound.

"Yes, I'm well aware." Worry twisted her pretty face. "You should sit. You were the one who was standing on a bomb." Her cheeks paled again.

He grabbed her hand. "I'm fine." The others entered the office. "And I have work to do. I need to find out who did this."

"Agreed," Killian said, as he strode in ahead of the others.

"Addie, I got you lunch." Devyn smiled, holding up a brown bag. "A fajita wrap from this place around the corner that Hex raves about. It's got chicken and lots of veggies. All good for you and the baby."

"Oh." Addie looked surprised. "Thank you, Devyn."

"Well, you guys missed your lunch date, and you need to eat." Devyn nudged Bram. "Plus, you're my bestie's girl, so that makes us besties, too."

Addie shot a startled look at Bram. Killian's phone rang, interrupting the moment. He walked away to answer it.

"Devyn only has one speed," Bram said. "But she's good people."

The redhead smiled. "I'll grow on you."

"Like a parasite," Bram added.

Devyn laughed and elbowed him. "Look at you, making a joke."

Killian ended his call, his hawkish face serious. "That was Matteo. He questioned Farley."

Bram flexed a hand. He liked the Irishman, even if he was a bit different. If the guy had set him up…

"Matteo said he was genuinely upset and horrified. He thought it was just a sensor malfunction and called it in. That was it."

"Someone had been in before the sensor problem started," Bram said. "Someone who deactivated the system, planted the bomb, then re-activated the system. They knew that if the sensor malfunctioned, then Farley would call me."

"Bram was the target," Addie whispered.

"It could've been to give this fucker easier access to Addie," Bram said. "Take me out, and leave Addie vulnerable."

"So this person deactivated our security system." Hex folded her arms and looked like a pissed-off fairy. "No way."

"Maybe he got someone's code?" Killian suggested. "A gallery employee."

A phone rang on the desk, and Hex snatched it up. "Hello? Okay. Yes, bring it down." She looked up. "A letter's been delivered to Bram by courier. The receptionist upstairs said we need to see it."

Moments later, the letter was delivered. Bram tore the white envelope open.

There were words and letters cut out from a newspaper, and stuck in the center of the white paper.

Boom, motherfucker.

I'll get you next time.

Adaline is mine.

Molten rage poured through Bram. His anger was white hot.

"Bram?" Addie stated.

He handed the note to Killian and his boss scowled.

"I want to see it." Addie strode forward.

"No," Bram said.

"Yes." She took it, read it, and all the color left her

cheeks. "You were the target. He wants to kill you because of me. This is all my fault."

Bram shoved the note at Hex, then pulled Addie close. He cupped her cheeks. "It's not your fault. This sick fuck is to blame. He's *not* going to lay a hand on you."

She grabbed Bram's wrists. "I don't want him to hurt you, either."

"No one is getting hurt," Killian said.

"Only the asshole," Devyn said. "Once we find the asshole."

"Then we'll shut him down for good." Killian nodded. "Now, let's get to work."

"I'm on the note," Nick said. "I'll take it to the lab."

"I'll pull CCTV at Farley's gallery," Hex said. "See what pops."

"I'll talk to Santi," Bram said. "See if he can get anything off the bomb."

"I want to help too," Addie said.

"You should rest," Bram said.

"No." She lifted her chin. "I'm not lying around. I'll just worry. I need to *do* something. This is *my* life. This man is after me." She turned. "I'm actually pretty decent on a computer. I did some computer studies at school."

"I could use you." Hex caught Bram's gaze over Addie's head.

He knew Hex would keep her here, safe. He nodded.

"I promise you it will be boring," Hex said.

"I don't care," Addie said. "I want to help stop this man."

"I think I'll visit some friends," Devyn said. "See if I can scare up some information."

Who knew what contacts the ex-CIA agent had? Bram realized his teammates were rallying around him. Helping him take care of Addie.

The center of Bram's chest tightened. He met Killian's gaze, held it.

His boss' lips quirked. "Let's get to work."

Bram watched Hex get Addie settled at a desk in the command center, showing her how to access the computer system. They pulled up CCTV of the gallery and the street around it.

"I warned you," Hex said. "It's going to be tedious."

"It's important," Addie said. "I want to help find this guy. He's terrified me, and now he almost killed Bram..."

Bram rested a hand on her shoulder and squeezed. She was worried about him. It'd been a long time since someone had cared for him like that.

Sure, his team had his back, but no one got a worried look and nibbled their bottom lip like this. Not since his ma and Fiona. He was pretty sure his dad didn't give a shit.

Bram pulled out his phone and wandered to the edge of the room. Hex gently bullied Addie into eating, and she started searching the CCTV footage. She had a cute little furrow in her brow as she concentrated.

His hand curled. He wanted to kiss that spot. Wanted to kiss her all over.

He remembered every detail of that long, dancer's body. He wanted her so much.

Keep her safe first.

He put the phone to his ear and called Santi.

"Excalibur. You doing okay?" the bomb expert rasped.

"Still alive and in one piece, thanks to you."

Santi snorted. "A good way to be, believe me, I know."

He remembered Santi's injuries. "Sorry."

"I'm alive and kicking, too. Could be worse. How's your pretty blonde? She looked freaked."

Bram glanced at Addie. "She's fine now."

"Baby yours?" Santi asked.

Bram released a deep breath. "Yeah."

"Congrats, man." He let out a laugh. "If it's a little girl who looks like her mama, you're so screwed."

Bram froze, his scowl deepening. A little girl? Wonder and fear mingled in his gut. He knew nothing about little girls. *Fuck.* He'd had a sister, and he'd failed in looking after her.

"Fuck."

Santi laughed. "When the boys come sniffing around—"

Bram cleared his throat. "I called about the bomb. Have you found anything."

"Standard IED, Bram. Put together with whatever our asshole could lay his hands on. Only one part I found that was of any interest."

Bram's hand tightened on the phone. "Yeah?"

"Yeah. One bit of metal had writing on it. A manufacturer part number. Might be nothing. He could have just found it in a scrap yard."

"What was it?"

"Not sure. The letters are in Cyrillic."

Bram frowned. "Russian?"

"Yes. But like I said, your bomber could've just raided a scrapyard or something. Might mean nothing."

Or it might mean something.

"Thanks, Santi. I'll even buy you that tequila you like."

Santi laughed. "I could choke down a decent whiskey. Take care of your girl, Excalibur."

"I plan to."

SHE WAS TIRED.

Addie's eyes were gritty, her back ached, and even her fingers were exhausted.

Hex had been right. Wading through CCTV footage was boring.

She rubbed the back of her neck. She wanted to help. She needed to be a part of finding out who was trying to destroy her life.

And hurt Bram.

Her stomach squeezed tight. She'd searched through footage from the gallery.

There had been nothing out of the ordinary until the internal cameras went dark for thirty minutes, when presumably her stalker had planted the bomb.

For Bram.

She gripped the arms of her chair.

He's fine. He's alive, Addie.

She knew he was in Killian's office, but suddenly, she really wanted to see him. She took a deep breath.

"Okay?" Hex appeared, sitting on the desk beside Addie's computer screen.

"I haven't found anything helpful."

"I told you it can be mind-numbing." Hex lifted a huge mug of coffee and sipped. "It takes time. And patience." She looked at the screen. "And you're right, you're pretty good with computers."

Addie felt a small flush of pride. "Thanks. It was the only thing I was good at when I was at school, apart from dancing."

"You've always wanted to be a dancer?" Hex asked.

"I..." Addie frowned. "Actually, I always just wanted to escape and make something of my life. We didn't have much money, my parents were always working, and I have five brothers and sisters."

Hex's eyes popped wide. "Five? Wow. I'm an only child, so that's hard to imagine. Are you close?"

Addie shook her head. "A couple of my brothers are into drugs." She sighed. "My sister is already married and doesn't talk to the family much. Everyone just went their separate ways." She'd tried to stay in touch with her siblings, but none of them were interested. "I thought dancing was my ticket to stardom." She gave Hex a sad smile. "It didn't quite work out the way I planned."

"Bram told me that you're an amazing dancer."

Addie flushed. "He said he came to some of my shows." She fiddled with her hair. "I felt almost guilty saying this. "After the last few years, the grind of auditions, training and practice, never making enough money to pay the bills..." She shrugged. "Dancing stopped being fun a long time ago."

Hex touched her hand. "I'm sorry."

"After I was abducted with Saskia, I guess I started to reevaluate things. Now I'm not sure what I want."

"Or maybe now you know dancing isn't your dream, you need to work out what is," Hex said.

Addie bit her lip. "Now, this baby needs to be my focus."

"Yes, but you don't have to lose yourself in the process." Hex looked at the screens. "And getting you safe needs to be the first priority." The hacker frowned. "Your stalker deactivated the cameras. He has bomb-making skills, and clearly some tech skills. He's not just your average Joe."

A shiver skated down Addie's spine. "So, who is he?"

Hex gripped her arm. "We'll find him. Don't worry. Bram won't give up." She cocked her head. "His code-name from his days in the Irish special forces was Excalibur. Because he was so honest and straightforward. Like King Arthur, who wielded the sword Excalibur. He protects, and he will always do what's right. And for you, I think he'd do anything." Hex paused. "He needs you, Addie. After so much pain, he deserves some softness. Some goodness."

"Pain?" Addie clenched the arms of her chair harder. Bram wasn't a talker, and she could tell he held a lot inside.

Hex pulled a face. "It's not my story to tell." She squeezed Addie's arm. "I'm glad he's got you. That he's let you in. There's a good guy under the grump." Then she peered at the computer screen. "Look. Across the street from the gallery."

"Yes, this was one of the images I wanted to show you," Addie said.

"When was this?" Hex asked.

"About an hour before the bomb was planted."

"The man's hanging in the doorway of the building across the street. He's watching the gallery."

"Waiting." Addie leaned forward, frustration hitting her. "He's only partly in the shot, and wearing a ball cap. I can't see him clearly."

"Wait." Hex's fingers flew across the keyboard. "I'll see if there are any cameras on the building where he's standing."

"How long will it take you to get access to that?"

"Oh, sweet Addie." Hex smiled. "I'm not asking permission."

"You're hacking in?" Addie leaned forward.

"Aha." The tech guru tapped a key with a flourish. "Sometimes you have to be a little bad to be good."

"Do I even want to know?" Killian's dry voice came from behind them.

Killian and Bram stood in the arched doorway. Addie's gaze went straight to Bram, and she stared at his rugged face. She wondered again what pain he had from his past.

She wanted him to share, to open up to her, and trust her.

"Got him!" Hex cried. "Here is the sketchy dude staring at the gallery, just before the bomb was planted."

Addie gasped.

"He's a big guy," Killian noted.

"Looks like he's the same height and weight as the

guy who broke into Addie's apartment." Bram crossed his arms.

Addie rose, staring at the man's image on the big screen. She couldn't see his face, just a bit of his jaw. *Who was he?*

"And we know he has bomb and tech skills," Hex added.

"I spoke to Santi," Bram said. "Parts of the bomb were stamped with Cyrillic letters." He scowled. "I heard the guy curse under his breath when I was fighting him at Addie's. I didn't pick it up at the time, but I'm pretty sure he cursed in Russian."

"Russian?" A wave of dizziness hit Addie.

She heard a commotion, and the room spun, then she was in Bram's arms.

He lowered her to a chair. "Easy."

Images from her abduction peppered her like rocks. She remembered being drugged, transported to that estate outside San Francisco. Saskia had been the main target of the wealthy, Russian businessman, and Addie had just been caught up in the chaos. In the wrong place at the wrong time. Story of her life.

She'd been terrified. She'd known her family wouldn't know where she was, or even if she was missing. Even if they knew, they would never have found her.

Thankfully, Killian Hawke had come for his sister. At that estate, other trafficked women had been forced to be the playthings of powerful men. Addie swallowed. It'd almost happened to her.

"Hey, sunshine." Bram knelt in front of her. "You're safe."

She grabbed his hand. "I know." She took a deep breath. "So, this man is Russian? Could Yaroslav Mikhailov be after me again?"

"Mikhailov is gone," Killian said. "He'll never cause you problems again."

"He was handed over to the CIA." Bram's face lightened. "I believe it was Devyn who took him off Killian's hands."

Killian frowned. "I would've preferred him dead."

Bram looked back at the screen. "We don't know who this guy is yet, but we're closing in."

"And you helped, Addie." Hex pointed at the screen. "You found this image. We don't have a full face, but I'll still try and run him through facial recognition."

Addie's stomach grumbled, and with a hiss, she pressed a hand to her belly.

Bram froze. "What's wrong?"

She smiled. "Nothing. I'm just hungry again. I have an insane craving for cookie dough ice cream." She cleared her throat. "And salt-and-vinegar chips."

"I love both those things," Hex said.

"Um, but I actually want them together. The chips in the ice cream."

Hex shuddered. "Ew. Pregnancy cravings are weird."

"Why don't we head up to my place," Bram said. "You can rest and I'll organize dinner."

She smiled at him. "Okay."

Hex looked at him askance. "You're going to cook?"

Bram grunted. "Hell, no. I'm going to order delivery." He glanced at Addie. "I can't cook."

"That's all right." She held onto his hand as she rose. "I can."

He gave her a faint smile. "I always enjoyed your baking."

God, a smile. A real smile. She wanted to see him do that more often.

"You're not cooking tonight." He slid an arm around her. "You're resting."

She loved his overprotective grumpiness. Too many times in her life, she'd felt on her own, and even unsafe. She'd done everything she could to be independent and look after herself, but a part of her loved knowing that this big, strong man was looking out for her.

Even if he was only doing it for the baby.

"If I find anything else, I'll let you know," Hex said.

CHAPTER EIGHT

B ram shifted on the couch, scrunching the pillow under his head to get more comfortable.

It was late. Addie had gone to bed hours ago, after he'd fed her Italian. He'd gotten a lot of satisfaction watching her enjoy the food. A few times, he'd gotten hard too, listening to her moaning, and savoring it.

Just thinking of her now, asleep in his bed...

He readjusted his pajama pants and grunted. She'd been so afraid earlier, when he'd been on that bomb.

But she hadn't left him.

And she'd wanted to help. Hex said she'd done a good job, and had an eye for the CCTV images.

He would've preferred she stay in the apartment and rest, but after seeing the way she'd relaxed by being involved, he was happy for her to help. Safely, from the command center.

He scowled at the ceiling, the city lights flickering in from around the curtains.

They still didn't have a name. It wasn't Mikhailov.

The asshole was locked up in a CIA black ops site and would never be seen again. Devyn had assured him of that.

Besides Mikhailov had been obsessed with Saskia, not Addie.

I will find you, asshole. You're not hurting her.

Suddenly, he heard Addie cry out from the bedroom.

He leaped up, throwing the blanket off and grabbed his Glock off the coffee table. He sprinted down the hallway and burst into the bedroom.

It was dark, but the light was on in the bathroom, so he could see well enough. There was no intruder. Just Addie sitting upright in the middle of the bed.

"Addie?"

She let out a small sob. "Sorry... I..." Another sob. "I had a nightmare. It was so real. I was back at that estate, locked in a room." Her voice shook. "I could hear the woman next door crying. And one of the guards chewed gum. I can still smell it. Like cinnamon."

"You're safe. You're in New York." Bram moved to the bed, and set his handgun down on the bedside table.

"I know," she whispered. "The nightmare just crept up on me." Her voice hitched. "Why would someone do this? Hunt me? Try to kill you? It's crazy."

He reached out and touched her silky hair.

She gripped his hand. "Bram, please, will you hold me?"

Damn. He couldn't risk getting in the same bed as her. His control around her was already dangerously thin.

"Please."

He couldn't say no to her. Not when he heard the plea in her voice. Not when she was afraid, and she needed him.

He climbed onto the bed and leaned against the headboard. He reached for her, but she was already climbing into his arms.

He pulled her close and she rested her face against his bare chest, wrapping her arms around him.

She was shaking and he stroked her back.

"That this guy might be Russian...I guess it brought back my abduction. It was the scariest thing that ever happened to me."

"I know, sunshine." He rubbed the base of her neck. He was conscious of her belly pressed against his abs. "You're safe now."

"I know," she murmured. "I've never felt safer than when I'm with you."

Feck. His chest tightened. "When you were younger...you didn't feel safe?"

He felt her shrug, nuzzling against his chest. He gritted his teeth, trying not to get hard.

"We didn't have a lot of money. My mom worked two jobs, and was always tired. To be honest, she just never showed much interest in us. I mean, there was always food. She did the best she could. Dad drank. He wasn't violent, but he was mostly absent. My siblings and I were left on our own a lot."

His hand tightened. "Did anyone hurt you?"

"No, Bram." She kissed his chest.

He rolled his eyes to the ceiling and tried to think of anything but her warm, soft lips on his skin.

"What was your childhood like?" she asked. "Back in Ireland?"

Something inside him stilled and his throat tightened. "Normal."

Silence fell in the room.

"I know your mom died," she said quietly. "Are you close to your dad?"

"No." It was hard work to force the word out.

"If you don't want to talk about it with me, that's fine."

Her tone was soft and even, but he was an expert in all things Addie. He heard the hurt she was trying to hide.

He blew out a breath. "My ma and little sister died." He gritted his teeth, flashes of the horror he tried never to remember hitting him like acid, chewing on his heart.

She gasped. "I'm sorry. How old were you?"

"Eighteen. I was just finishing school." Afterward, he'd joined the military. "Da isn't a man of many words. And with my mother and sister gone..." Things had been awkward. Neither of them had talked. Bram had been grieving and feeling guilty. His father's silence had just made him angrier.

"I'm so sorry, Bram. How old was your sister?"

He thought of a wide smile, uneven pigtails. "She was twelve. Fiona. Her name was Fiona."

She'd screamed his name as she was being dragged away.

"Bram? Bram?"

Warm fingers touched his jaw. He blinked. Addie was watching him, worry on her face.

"I'm sorry I made you go somewhere dark," she said.

"It was a long time ago."

"And some old hurts fade, but they never go away."

He knew that truth better than anyone.

"I thought I'd put the abduction by Mikhailov behind me." She rubbed her cheek against Bram's chest. "This brought it all up again."

He pulled her closer. "It's normal, Addie. But I don't want you to worry. It's not good for the baby." He moved his hand toward her stomach, then paused.

She pulled it the rest of the way and he cupped her belly, over where their child grew.

"My brain knows I'm safe now." She pressed a hand over his heart, toying with the hair on his chest. "I guess I'm just waiting for the rest of me to catch up."

The caress was torture. He stifled a groan and thought of the harsh training he'd gone through in the military to keep his body under control.

"I will find this asshole, Addie. I promise."

"As long as you stay safe, too."

He grunted. He'd do what he had to do. Once, he hadn't been able to do anything to save the people he loved.

He wouldn't let it happen again with Addie.

"I should go and let you get some sleep," he said.

Her hands tightened. "Please stay."

It would be more torture. Staying in bed, holding her. He'd risk giving into things he shouldn't. "You'll sleep better without me."

"That's not true. I...I don't want the nightmare to come back. I know it won't if you're here with me."

Bram sighed and slid a hand into her hair. "All right, sunshine. Sleep now."

She sighed, relaxing against him, her hand over his heart.

Desire thrummed through him, but he held her. It was worth every bit of torture.

WAKING SLOWLY, Addie stretched her arms over her head. She felt warm and cozy. She could smell Bram.

Bram.

She remembered the nightmare. It didn't seem so bad now, in the light of the morning. Bram had held her in those strong arms the rest of the night. It had felt so right.

He was gone now. She opened her eyes and saw the indent in the pillow beside her and stretched her arm out. The sheets were cool.

She bit her lip. He'd stayed with her because she'd begged him. Her chest tightened. He'd protect her, look after her, because he was a good guy, and she was pregnant.

But it didn't mean he wanted her.

Her mother's words echoed in her head.

Never trust a man, Adaline. They get what they want, and then they lose interest. It's just a fact of life.

Her legs twisted in the sheets, her body hot. His hard body had been pressed against hers, and she'd felt the strength of his chest, covered in that light dusting of red hair.

He was so big, solid, manly. He made her feel so small and feminine.

Those ten days when he'd shared her bed, he'd wanted her. He hadn't been able to get enough of her. Every night, he'd come to her place, and he'd get her naked as fast as possible.

Wherever she was, he'd take her. He'd spread her on the couch, and put his head between her legs until she'd been sweaty and screaming. Once, he'd fucked her hard on the kitchen counter while breakfast burned in the pan. He'd taken her roughly against the wall.

She'd loved the force of his need, like he couldn't get enough of her.

Now, he hesitated any time he touched her.

Addie was starting to realize her dreams had shifted and changed. While dancing would always be important to her, being a star and dancing on stage wasn't what she wanted.

She wanted to be the best mother she could. She rubbed circles on her belly. And she wanted Bram.

Her skin felt flushed, her belly heavy. Damn, hormones.

She sat up, then headed for the bathroom. She washed up and pulled on her cute robe over her T-shirt. She was wearing another one of Bram's shirts. She pushed her hair back and went in search of him.

He wasn't in the living room or kitchen. She frowned. Maybe he'd gone into the office early.

Then she heard a sound from the second bedroom. She wandered down the hall and found the door ajar. She peered through the crack.

He was still shirtless. That gave her a little thrill. Her gaze ran over the slabs of muscle and large biceps.

Addie swallowed. His black pajama pants rode low on his hips. He sat on a stool, mostly in profile to her. His hands were moving.

On the table in front of him was... She blinked. A block of wood. He was carving.

Addie straightened and pushed the door open, drawn in.

Bram's head shot up, his hand stilling. "Addie."

"Good morning." Her gaze dropped to those scarred hands on that smooth brown wood. "What are you doing?"

"Um." He looked uncomfortable. "Nothing."

"It doesn't look like nothing." There were lots of tools resting on the table. They looked to be good quality, and well used. Then she turned and sucked in a breath.

There were several shelves on the wall and they were all filled with wooden carvings. The sculptures were beautiful. She walked closer, Bram's silence deafening.

Some were just abstract shapes—interesting twists and whirls of smooth wood. One was a lion sitting, looking majestic. Another a hawk perched on a branch, each feather intricately carved.

Then she saw the dancer. It was a woman in a tutu in mid-pirouette à la seconde. Her elegant hand was raised in front of her.

Addie's heart thumped hard. The face had been carved in glorious detail.

It was *her*.

The next carving was her, as well. She was standing,

a thin dress clinging to her body. She looked beautiful, ethereal.

The next one she was sitting, her long hair over her shoulder as she brushed it. She had a serene look on her face. Another was her standing in the wind, her hair and long dress blowing up behind her, making her look like a goddess.

And there was another one of her dancing. It was a moment from her show.

In every one she looked beautiful, special.

Is this how he saw her?

"You made these?" Her voice was thick.

"It's just a hobby."

She whirled. "It's more than a hobby, Bram. They're amazing. You're so talented."

Dull color filled his cheeks. "It's just a hobby," he insisted. "I'm self-taught."

She moved closer. "When did you start?"

"In high school. When I had the time. In the military." He shrugged a shoulder. "It was just something to do."

No, it was a passion. She spotted a statue of a young, smiling girl. It was a little rougher than the others.

He'd made it earlier than the others. Something clicked. "Is this Fiona?"

A pause. "Yes."

"You started carving your sister."

He was silent a moment. "Yes. After she was killed."

"Killed?" Addie's stomach clenched. "It wasn't an accident?"

"No." His tone said that he didn't want to talk about

it, but she could almost feel the throb of his pain. Her heart hurt for him.

Addie turned back to the shelves. "And these are all me." She touched one. The dress was so thin that it showed her nipples. She looked sensual. She glanced at him. "Is this how you see me?"

"You're so beautiful, Addie. It's easy to carve you."

She walked toward him, her pulse pounding in her ears, emotions whirling. "What are you carving now?"

"You again."

She touched the block of wood. "Your art is amazing, Bram."

He hunched his big shoulders. "It's just a hobby," he repeated. His tone dared her to argue.

"Will you show me?"

He gave her a reluctant nod. She realized he rarely said no to her.

He pulled her close and she sat on his lap. He stiffened, but then he picked up a tool. "I start by chiseling out a rough shape."

"Do you sketch it out first?"

"No. The images are in my head, and some details come to me as I carve."

She put her hand on the tool, his big hand closing over hers.

"The wood talks to you," she said.

He snorted. "Hardly."

Addie smiled. No, he was too down-to-earth. He wouldn't describe it that way.

Together they moved the tool, wood shavings peeling off.

She couldn't imagine being able to turn this lump of wood into anything as detailed as the art on the shelves. He moved her hand, his body surrounding hers. She shivered. This was intimate, sensual.

Swallowing, she felt her skin flush. She squirmed a little.

One of his hands clamped on her hip. "Addie." It was a low growl.

She felt the hard bulge beneath her, and her pulse spiked.

He was hard. He wanted her.

And she wanted him. So badly.

She shifted again, on purpose, rubbing her butt against his hard erection.

"*Addie*," he said in a warning tone.

"I need you, Bram. I'm hot, needy, and—" she turned her head "—so wet."

She saw the raw need on his rugged features. His hand slid from her hip to her thigh. He rubbed her skin.

"I promised myself that I wouldn't take advantage of you." His voice was gritty.

She gave a hiccupping laugh. "Even if I want you to? Even if I need you to?"

He groaned as his hand slid between her thighs. "You need me to touch you here?"

"*Yes*." She leaned back against him. His mouth moved to her neck, and his fingers pushed her panties aside.

He ran his knuckles against her. Addie cried out. When his fingers touched her clit, she moaned his name. "I've imagined you doing this so many times."

He pressed harder and she writhed.

"You are so beautiful. I love watching your face when I touch you." He stroked her folds. "I love that this sweet pussy gets so wet for me. What do you need, Addie?"

"*You*. I need to come."

With a deep growl, he rose. He set her on the table, shoved the wood aside, and pushed her backward. A second later, her panties were gone, and his mouth was on her.

"Bram!"

There was so much sensation shooting through her. She registered the scrape of his stubble on her inner thighs, his tongue lapping at her, his strong hands gripping her.

She arched up. "So good."

A thick finger slid inside her, and soon she was chanting his name. Her climax was building, and it was huge.

With another lick, she shattered. She cried out his name, her body shaking.

It felt like it went on forever. Finally, she slumped back, panting.

She heard him groan and she pushed up on her elbows.

His face was flushed, his mouth shining because of her. She bit her lip. As she watched, he shoved down his pajama pants and freed his cock.

Like the rest of him, it was thick and ruddy. He stroked it roughly.

"*Addie*." His hungry gaze met hers as he pumped his cock.

He was so sexy. "Come, Bram."

A second later, he did. His cock spurted onto the floor, as he groaned her name through his release.

Then there was only the sound of their fast breathing.

"Bram." She sat up, a little more awkwardly than she liked thanks to the baby. He helped her upright, and she kissed him.

It was slow, sensual. His lips moved over hers, and they took their time, his hands gripping her hard.

The sound of buzzing interrupted.

"That's my phone." He muttered and pulled it out. He dragged in a breath, gave Addie's arm a squeeze, then pressed the speaker button. "Hex."

"Morning, Bram. You and Addie get moving. I've got a lead for you. Tell Addie I have a breakfast sandwich for her. Get down here. Now."

CHAPTER NINE

When she walked into the Sentinel Security office, Addie was still flushed. Not from the shower she'd just taken, but from Bram.

Every second of what they'd done in that room kept playing through her head in glorious detail.

He'd wanted her. Desperately.

She'd loved every moment, especially watching him stroke his thick cock and watching him come.

She bit her lip and felt a pulse between her legs.

"You all right?" Bram asked.

"Um, yes. Just hungry." She fought back a blush. He was in one of his suits, and she never, ever got tired of seeing him dressed for work.

"There you two are." Hex spun in her chair. Killian was standing beside her.

"Morning," the head of Sentinel Security said.

Addie nodded, and saw Hex eyeing her and Bram, a faint smile on the hacker's face.

"Addie, here's breakfast for you." Hex brandished

something wrapped in white paper.

The smell of bacon and eggs made Addie's mouth water. "Thanks, Hex."

"What did you find?" Bram asked.

"It might be nothing, so don't get too excited yet." Hex jerked a thumb at Killian. "The boss man's contacts came through. A Russian businessman here in New York —" her nose wrinkled "—and I use the term businessman lightly—might have intel on our guy."

"Sergei Limonov owns some clubs in Brooklyn," Killian said. "He's an okay guy, always eager to stay on my good side."

Addie couldn't imagine ever being on Killian's bad side. She fought back a shiver.

"I'll pay him a visit," Bram said.

Killian lifted his chin. "I'll go with you."

"And Addie, I have more riveting CCTV for you to wade through," Hex said. "And to liven things up a little, I'll show you how to hack into a locked cell phone."

"Whatever I can do to help." Addie's heart knocked in her chest. She looked at Bram. "You'll be safe?"

His lips quirked. "Yes, sunshine. I can take care of myself, and I'll have Killian with me."

Killian nodded. "I'll have his back. Plus, Devyn will probably meet us. She's out doing something, but will join us once she's finished."

Bram pressed a kiss to Addie's forehead. "Stay with Hex."

Addie nodded.

"I'll see you when I get back."

Then they were gone.

"You've got the look of a woman who spent the morning in bed with a big, sexy hunk of an Irishman," Hex said.

Addie's cheeks flamed and she sat, rubbing her belly. She took a bite of her breakfast sandwich. She hadn't had a chance to make close girlfriends after she'd moved to New York, so she never gossiped about men or dating with anyone. She'd started from scratch after leaving home, and dancing had kept her busy. It was also a cutthroat world, so she hadn't really bonded with any other dancers. She'd met Saskia during their ordeal, but afterward, the other woman had fallen in love with her hot guy and moved to San Francisco. They talked on the phone, but it wasn't the same.

"Um, not in bed," Addie said.

"Ooh, so Bram can get creative, huh? I wouldn't have pegged him for that."

"We've fooled around, but... We haven't gone all the way."

Hex cocked her head. "But you want to."

"Yes." She clenched her hands. "He's holding back. I think he's just looking out for me because I'm pregnant and he feels obligated."

Hex laughed. "That's not it."

"It isn't?"

"No. You've been through a lot. You're pregnant. That was a shock for both of you. He's feeling off balance and he knows you must be, too. Especially with this stalker thing. He's a good guy, Addie. He won't take advantage."

"He did say that, but I want him to take advantage."

Hex grinned. "So, it's up to you. You need to seduce your baby daddy."

Seduce him? Hot flames licked Addie's belly at the thought. But she'd never seduced anyone in her life.

"Think about it." Hex pointed at the computer screen. "Now, get to work."

Soon, she was busy with the searches. There was no sign of the big stalker who was after her. Hex showed her a few things on the computer, and Addie felt a little thrill. She enjoyed computer work.

"Okay, let's take a short break and I'll show you how to get into a locked cellphone." Hex held up a sleek phone. "Ready?"

"Ready."

Following Hex's instructions, it wasn't long before Addie unlocked the phone. She grinned.

"You're a natural." Hex grinned back and pointed at the screen. "That's the Sentinel Security emergency number. The team can call or message it anywhere in the world, and it comes straight to me."

"Don't you ever take a vacation?"

"Nope. I love my work too much."

"You're amazing at this."

Hex executed a little bow. "I accept all manner of flattery and fawning adulation."

Addie laughed and turned back to the computer to check her searches. Her mind kept drifting to Bram. Had he found anything? Was he okay?

"Hex, have you got a boyfriend?" she asked.

"Me? No way. Men are often more trouble than they're worth. I'll exclude all the guys I work with, but they're all taken now, and unfortunately, I've never felt the urge to bang any of them." She shook her head. "I've always been smart, and unlike some leggy dancers I know, small and cute." She wrinkled her nose. "Men like legs, and curves, and boobs, none of which I have."

"You're gorgeous!"

Hex grinned. "Aw, you are so sweet." Her smile faded. "There was a guy. After I graduated college. I thought we were headed somewhere serious...until he dumped me for a wannabe model. He said he just didn't 'want me that way.'"

"He sounds horrible." Addie sensed a deeper hurt under Hex's words.

The other woman shrugged. "I've never been in love. Guys usually let me down." She smiled. "I can be an acquired taste. One day, I hope I find some guy who rocks my world, but I'm not settling for less." Her tone was vehement. "Ever. Changing things about yourself to suit another person...? No way."

Bram almost seemed to worship everything Addie did. He never, ever wanted her to change, and he didn't put her down. Now that she'd learned that he'd snuck into her dance shows, multiple times, to watch her, she felt a little giddy. Little, warm pops filled her belly. She pressed a palm there and frowned. She could almost feel the pops. Was it the baby?

The thud of footsteps caught her ear, and Bram appeared. He had a scowl in place.

God, she loved that grumpy look. It made her want to kiss him.

"No luck?" Hex asked.

Bram shook his head. "We showed Limonov the pics, but he couldn't identify the man. He thought maybe he'd seen him. That he was muscle for somebody." Bram set a bag down on the desk in front of Addie.

"What's this?"

"I got you something."

She opened it and gasped in delight. "Cookie dough ice cream, and salt-and-vinegar chips." She hurriedly opened the ice cream, then tore open the chips and tipped them in. She grabbed a spoon and took a mouthful. Sweet and salty and crunchy. *Yum.*

Hex watched in horror. "So gross."

Addie just moaned. She took another mouthful and smiled at Bram. He smiled back.

That smile softened the rugged lines of his face.

She swallowed. "Um, I have a doctor's appointment this afternoon. The ultrasound. Are you coming?"

His smile flattened. "Yes."

"Oh, how exciting," Hex said. "You'll get to see if it's a boy or girl. If you want to find out."

Bram looked faintly green.

"Yes, I think I do want to find out," Addie said.

"I'll go make a few calls," Bram said. "Nick is going to tail us to the appointment. Make sure it's safe."

"Go out the back entrance of the warehouse," Hex suggested.

"You don't have to come," Addie told him. "If you're too busy." She didn't want him to be uncomfortable.

His jaw tightened. "I'm coming."

HE'D FACED DOWN armed bad guys.

He'd gone into battle.

He'd been under fire numerous times.

But he'd never been this nervous. Bram walked Addie through the doors of the doctor's office, a hand pressed to her lower back, and resisted the urge to tug on the neckline of his shirt.

There were lots of pregnant women in varying stages. One woman's stomach looked so large he couldn't believe she wasn't toppling over.

As Addie spoke to the receptionist, he looked at a poster on the wall. It was showing something called cervical dilation. He blinked at it in horror, a wave of dizziness hitting him.

"Bram?"

He jerked back to look at Addie. She was lowering herself into a seat. He sat beside her and stared at the blank wall.

Her hand touched his. "You okay?"

"Fine."

"You don't look fine."

He glanced at her. "The guys at the office think I have the best poker face."

"Not to me." She squeezed his fingers. "People have babies every day, Bram. It's going to be fine."

The thought of Addie actually having the baby made his chest lock. The thought of her in pain...

No.

In fact, people died during childbirth didn't they? His pulse kicked up a gear.

"Bram, breathe."

The air rushed into him.

"Adaline Harris?" a nurse called.

Bram followed Addie into a room. There was a bunk, and a fancy machine with a large screen beside it.

"Lie up on the bed, and put the sheet over your lower body," the nurse said. "Dr. Choudhury will be in soon."

Bram helped Addie up on the bed and get settled, then he pulled a chair over. He tried not to fidget.

"Hello." A woman in her early thirties bounced in. She was curvy with a wide smile, short, black hair, and dark-brown skin. Something about her energy reminded him of Hex.

"How are you today, Addie?

"Fine, thanks, Dr. Choudhury." Addie smiled. "And this is Bram. He's the father of the baby."

"Don't worry, daddy, there's nothing to be nervous about." The doctor pushed Addie's shirt up. "We're going to take a little look at your bub, make sure everything is good."

His gaze snagged on Addie's cute baby bump covered in smooth skin.

"The gel will be a little cool," the doctor warned.

"It's fine." Addie drew a breath. "I'm excited. And nervous."

Bram took her hand.

"Relax." The doctor moved the wand over Addie's belly. "Okay, let's take a little look."

Bram stared at the screen. It was all black and gray shadows, and he couldn't make any sense of them.

"All right, here we go. There's your baby."

Bram stared. He saw it now—head, body, legs kicking.

His heart pounded in his chest. A baby. A real baby.

"Oh, look, Bram." Addie's voice was delighted. She squeezed his fingers, and he squeezed back.

It was just a tiny thing. They'd made it. It was resting safely there in Addie's belly.

A fierce wave of protectiveness hit him.

He'd keep them both safe. No matter what.

Suddenly, it hit him that eventually the baby would be born, and out in the world with all its dangers. His other hand curled into a fist.

"Do you want to know if you're having a boy or a girl?" Dr. Choudhury asked.

Bram couldn't breathe. He looked at Addie, saw the shining look in her eyes.

He nodded.

"Yes, please," Addie said.

"Well, you're having a little girl," Dr. Choudhury said.

Okay, now it felt like the world had stopped. Or a bomb had gone off.

A girl.

A baby girl.

He didn't know anything about little girls. His mouth was dry. He thought of Fiona, heard the echo of her laugh. She'd love this—seeing him rattled and knowing that she'd be an aunt.

Addie squeezed his hand again, her eyes teary, but she was smiling. "We've got this. Together."

Tension eased from him. Addie would help him learn what he needed to know.

Then the doctor tensed and leaned forward.

"What's wrong?" he demanded.

"Hang on." The doctor was frowning.

Addie bit her lip and he smoothed a hand up her arm.

"Is something wrong with the baby?" Addie's voice trembled.

The doctor smiled. "No. It's just something that got missed previously, because we thought you were measuring ahead based on the father's size. Baby A is perfectly healthy."

"Baby A?" Bram frowned, and saw another bubble appear on the screen.

Addie gasped.

"Congratulations. You're having twins."

"Two?" Bram just stared dumbly at the screen. "There are two?"

"Oh my gosh." Addie's fingers tightened, her face pale. "How could we not know?"

"It happens sometimes," Dr. Choudhury said. "The second baby is missed in the early scan." The doctor's smile was wide. "You're having a boy *and* a girl."

Addie made a choked sound.

This time, Bram needed to comfort her. He pressed a kiss to her for head. "Together, remember?" He had no idea how. He wasn't sure how to be a father to one baby, let alone two. "You're not alone."

She smiled, but it was a little shaky.

He couldn't stop from touching his lips to hers.

"Together," she whispered.

There were balls of knots in his gut. He couldn't fail her, but he had a history of letting the women in his life down.

His phone vibrated. As the doctor talked some more with Addie, he checked it. There was a message from Nick.

Time to move. Hex spotted an SUV out front. Could be nothing, but don't want to take any risks.

No, he wouldn't take risks with Addie. Or the babies.

Babies.

Jeez. He'd have to wrap his head around it later. For now, he'd get her safe.

CHAPTER TEN

How the hell was she going to seduce the father of her baby? Um, babies.

It still hadn't quite sunk in that she was pregnant with twins. A little boy and a little girl.

Addie chewed on the end of her pen, staring at the computer screen.

Bram was taking care of her and keeping her safe. But something was still holding him back. She was sure it had something to do with losing his mother and sister.

That he blamed himself.

"Earth to Addie?"

Hex's voice jerked her out of her thoughts. The other woman's brow was creased.

"You sure everything went okay at your doctor's appointment? The baby is okay?"

Addie licked her lips. She wasn't sure she should share the news without Bram. He was in the office somewhere with Killian and Devyn.

She didn't think he'd mind. "Babies. There are two."

Hex's mouth formed an O. "Twins?"

"Yes."

"Oh, my God." Hex squealed and threw her arms in the air. "Congratulations. That is amazing, and crazy." She sat on the desk, swinging her feet. "Holy cow, Bram with twins. I can't picture it."

"A boy and a girl." It still didn't feel real.

"No wonder you're looking shellshocked."

Addie shook her head. "It's not that." She rubbed a hand over her belly. "I mean, it's a surprise, but a good one. I worry about how we'll cope—"

Hex pressed a hand over Addie's. "You're not alone."

Emotion welled. "I know. But...I don't want Bram just because he feels duty-bound to me. I want him. All of him"

Hex's expression turned serious. "Okay, go on."

"I want him to love me, Hex. I want him to throw me on the bed and..." Her cheeks heated.

"I always wondered what Bram would be like in bed." Hex winked.

Addie laughed and pressed her hands to her cheeks. "He can be very focused, and a little rough, in a good way."

"Quit rubbing it in."

"But the last few days, he's been taking care of me, but he hasn't said how he feels..."

"Hmm, well talking about feelings isn't one of Bram's strengths."

Addie nodded and plucked at her shirt. "I know. He's holding back. He's made sure I've... Um..."

"He's given you some glorious orgasms." Hex grinned. "Lucky lady."

"But he hasn't made love to me."

"I told you, you definitely need to seduce him. Drive him so crazy that his rock-solid, Irish control snaps."

"What if he doesn't want me?"

"Pfft. He does."

"If I chase him, I might drive him away." Addie lowered her voice. "I can't lose him."

"Oh, you won't. That man is head over heels for you. Not just because you have his babies inside you."

"Babies?" Devyn sauntered in.

Killian's woman was so gorgeous and fit, her glorious, russet-red hair shining. It was up in a tight ponytail today. She had a tan-colored shirt tucked into fitted black pants. A gun was holstered on her belt. Just being in the same room with Devyn made Addie suddenly feel fat and frumpy.

"Bram and Addie are having twins," Hex said.

Devyn's eyebrows went up, then she smiled. "Congratulations, Addie. God, the big guy will lose his mind. I can imagine him cradling a baby girl. Wrestling a little boy."

Oh. Wonder hit Addie. She could picture that so clearly.

"The big guy won't do the business with Addie," Hex said.

"Hex!" More heat filled Addie's cheeks.

"Hmm." Devyn sat in a chair and crossed her long legs. "He's overprotective to the max. He's being consumed by guilt, knowing that you thought he ghosted you."

"But he wants you, Addie," Hex added. "So much it's making him crazy."

Devyn nodded. "That's a given."

"You think?" Addie asked.

"Yep." Devyn's gaze narrowed. "And I think he'd do anything for you. Why don't you ask him for what you want?"

"I can't order him to..."

"Fuck you hard and make you scream?" Devyn suggested.

Hex laughed, and Addie clapped her hands to her cheeks.

"That man would do anything for you," Devyn added quietly.

"But I want him to do it because he wants to."

Devyn smiled. "I really don't think you have to worry about that."

Hex nodded.

Addie needed to mull it over. Could she demand Bram make love to her? Just the thought left her feeling shivery.

"So, I actually have news." Devyn's face turned serious.

"What?" Hex asked.

"Pam," the redhead said darkly.

"She's gone," Hex said." You can't go all Hellfire on her and kill her."

Addie blinked. "Kill her?" She turned to Devyn. "She's joking, right?"

"No," Devyn said, face bland.

Addie felt like she was getting a glimpse of the CIA spy, the woman who could go toe-to-toe with Killian Hawke.

"Pam was fired," Hex said. "She's out. Done. *Finito*."

"I found evidence that our friend Pammy got several large payments into her bank account, around the time Addie came into the Sentinel Security looking for Bram," Devyn said.

"What?" Hex flew to her computer and started tapping.

"I suspect she's in contact with someone else who didn't want Addie and Bram re-connecting," Devyn added.

"My stalker?" Addie breathed.

Devyn nodded. "I think so. Sorry."

"Fuck," Hex snapped. "I see the transfers came from a Caymans bank account. It'll take me a while to trace them, and I'll check phone records, too. And Addie, I'm sending CCTV from Pam's apartment building to your computer. See if she meets with anybody that you recognize."

Addie nodded, feeling slightly confused and overwhelmed. "I'm not special. Why would someone come after me like this?"

"You're beautiful, sweet, and kind," Hex said. "That's pretty special."

Devyn nodded. "Sweet and kind are rare commodities."

Addie touched her computer screen. Images began to pop up. One showed Pam coming out of her apartment.

She flicked through more. Pam with a fancy handbag. Pam lugging grocery bags. Pam stopping on the street and talking to a tall man right outside her front door. The man had his back to the camera.

Addie frowned. The way he moved...

Then he turned, and she gasped.

"Addie?" Devyn leaned forward. "What is it?"

"I recognize this man." A cold shiver made her feel like her skin had been coated in ice. She'd never forget the man's frosty, intense gaze.

"He was a Russian guard at Mikhailov's estate in the Napa Valley. He was the guard on my room."

"He matches the size and height of the attacker from your apartment," Hex said.

"Bingo," Devyn said.

***

BRAM STRODE INTO THE OFFICE, his blood boiling.

Several images up on the big, interactive screen showed a tall, tough-faced motherfucker.

The man had flat cheeks, a crooked nose that had been broken a few times, and a heavy jaw. Bram glared at the man's dark-brown eyes.

Yep, this was him. The man who thought he could take Addie. Scare her. Hurt her.

"Who is he?" Bram barked.

Hex spun. "Cool it down, Excalibur."

"No."

Addie stood off to the side, her arms wrapped around her middle, her face pale.

He instantly went to her. As soon as he opened his arms, she came to him and pressed her face to his chest.

"You recognize him?" Bram asked.

She nodded. "He was a guard at Mikhailov's estate. He never said anything to me, but he was...creepy. He stared. A lot."

And it had been enough to ignite an obsession.

"Hex, what have we got?" Killian strode in with Devyn and Nick.

"His name is Ilya Kozlov," Hex said. "Russian, was employed by Mikhailov."

"Why isn't he in jail, after his boss went down?" Bram asked.

"He gave evidence and took a deal." Hex pulled a face. "Then he disappeared."

"And became obsessed with Addie, and followed her here to New York," Bram said.

He felt her tremble, but she kept her gaze on the screen.

"Then the object of his obsession fell for another guy," Devyn said.

"And Kozlov stepped in to keep you apart," Hex said. "He paid Pam to keep you guys from connecting."

Bram's hands tightened on Addie. He'd been manipulated. He was angry at himself for falling for it. "Where is he now?"

He'd find Kozlov and end this. One way or another.

The man wasn't touching Addie. He wasn't scaring her anymore.

"I found his name on two leases in the city. An apartment in Brighton Beach, and a small storage space in Queens."

Addie's cellphone rang. She pulled it out and frowned. "I don't recognize the number."

Hex tapped on the keyboard. "Put it on speaker."

Addie nodded. "Hello?"

"Hello, my Adaline." The man had a thick, Russian accent.

She stiffened, and Bram's spine locked.

Hex made a motion with her hands. "I'll try to track him."

"It took me time to find your new number," Kozlov continued.

"Why are you stalking me?" Addie said.

"I'm not stalking you. I love you. I want to take care of you. You're so beautiful."

"You don't know me. I want you to leave me alone." Her voice rose.

Bram ran a hand down her back.

"I will know you. I will love you. I'll take very good care of you."

"I have a man and I'm pregnant with his babies."

"You should never have let him fuck you, Adaline." Kozlov's voice hardened. "You'll forget about him once you're with me, and I'm loving you."

Bram barely held back his growl.

"You can give the babies away," Kozlov continued. "Then I will put my babies in your belly."

Bram saw the fear and revulsion on her face. "Leave me alone!"

"I will find you soon, Adaline. Soon, we'll be together."

The line went dead.

"I'll go to his apartment," Killian said.

Nick nodded. "I'll come with you."

"Bram and I will check out the storage space," Devyn said.

Addie looked up. "Be careful."

"We will, sunshine." Bram cupped her jaw.

"Come back to me, Bram. To us."

He pressed a quick, hard kiss to her lips and pulled away. Devyn jerked her head. "Let's go, big guy."

———

THEY TOOK HIS TRUCK. Bram focused on driving and not the raging need to rip Kozlov's head off.

"You okay?" Devyn asked.

"No."

"You can't kill the guy." She paused. "Or at least you shouldn't. If you want to, I'll help you dispose of the body."

He glanced at her. He couldn't tell if she was serious or not. "I just want Kozlov stopped."

Devyn nodded. "So, let's stop him." She smiled. "Been too long since I was in a good fight."

He grunted. "You were in several last week."

"Like I said, too long."

When Bram parked the truck in front of the storage unit in Queens, he checked his Glock and tucked it into the holster under his jacket, then he and Devyn walked down the street. It was in an industrial area close to the rail lines.

The building looked like it had once been an old factory. They walked in like they belonged in the place.

"We're closing soon," a bored woman sitting at the reception desk said.

"We won't be long," Devyn said.

Devyn plugged in the code Hex had given them and they walked into the storage area. Ahead was a long row with roller doors on either side.

"No sign of Ilya Kozlov on CCTV," Hex said in their earpieces.

"We might find some evidence in his storage locker." Devyn's boot squeaked on the concrete floor.

Bram stared at the rows and rows of orange roller doors on the storage units.

"Take the next left," Hex said. "Unit 111. Three doors down."

They stopped at the right door, and he looked at the gleaming padlock.

"Bram, block the view of the camera," Devyn said quietly.

He swiveled, and watched as she pulled out a lock pick like he'd never seen before. A moment later, the padlock opened, and Devyn grinned.

"I have a magic touch with locks." She straightened. "We know this guy is handy with a bomb, so let's go cautiously."

Bram nodded and heaved the roller door open.

Devyn crouched and used the light on her phone to check the doorway. "Clear."

Bram clicked on the light in the storage unit.

Then he froze. It was like the air was sucked out of his lungs.

"Fuck me," Devyn murmured.

Bram took a step inside. The unit was mostly empty, except for a few boxes, and what covered the walls. The walls were covered in photos of Addie.

He turned his head, jaw tight. There were pictures of her on the street, shopping, dancing, working at the bar. Some were taken through her bedroom window as she changed her clothes.

His hands curled into fists.

"Take it easy." Devyn gripped his arm. "Dial it back. We need evidence to find the sick fuck."

They searched through the boxes. Bram took photos of the walls and Devyn collected a few bills and receipts, but there was nothing obvious. Nothing pointing to where Kozlov was hiding.

I will find you, asshole. Bram made the silent promise.

"Let's go," Devyn said. "The place is closing."

He gave her a short nod.

"When we get back to the office, we'll hit the gym. You can burn it off."

He grunted.

When they stepped outside, night was falling, and the street was empty. He heard the rumble of a train in the distance.

Then Devyn suddenly stopped. "Or maybe we'll burn it off now."

He lifted his head.

Four large silhouettes were waiting in the street by his truck.

One man held a steel bar in his hand, tapping it menacingly on his palm.

CHAPTER ELEVEN

B ram carefully scanned their surroundings, rage welling inside of him.

"Kozlov's friends, I assume," Devyn said, her voice cool.

"I doubt the asshole has friends," Bram muttered.

He and Devyn strode down the street.

Devyn raised her voice. "Kozlov send you?"

Bram gave a small shake of his head. That was Devyn, straight to the point.

"*Da,*" a man rumbled.

"Where is he?" Devyn continued.

"He does not want to be found." The man who spoke was muscular, with a puckered scar on his cheek, and a heavy Russian accent. "And he wants you to stay away from what's his." The man skewered Bram with a hard look.

"She isn't property," Bram said. "And she's pregnant with *my* babies. He's a fucking stalker—"

"Bram," Devyn murmured.

Right. He needed to keep his cool.

"Look boys, this won't go your way." Devyn pressed a hand to one hip. "Walk away now, and we won't hurt you."

The men stared at her for a beat, then started laughing.

"Whatever Kozlov paid you, it's not enough," she warned.

"Our boss owed him a favor, and we must pay it."

Another man smiled, eyeing Devyn hungrily. "You are just a woman." He rubbed his crotch. "Good for only one thing."

Oh, shit. Bram tensed. This wouldn't end well.

Devyn's smile turned sharp. "And an idiot like you is only good for one thing, too. I'll be happy to show you."

Fuck. Bram knew that Devyn was good in a fight, but if any of these assholes touched her, or she got hurt, Killian would lose his mind.

The Russians laughed, and Bram drew in a breath. They weren't Kozlov, but they were helping the fucker. Bram had plenty of rage to work off.

The man with the scar muttered something in Russian. The guy with the crowbar came at Bram. He swung the bar fast.

Bram ducked, then spun. He landed a hard punch to the man's mid-section. The guy grunted, and Bram ripped the bar free of his hands. He turned and hit the guy hard in the head.

The man dropped to the ground.

Devyn launched forward. The smart-mouthed man came at her, grinning.

He didn't grin for long. Devyn's kick hit him straight in the face. He yowled, and she followed through with two hard punches, and an elbow to his throat.

As he gagged, her front kick toppled him over.

Bram whirled on the other two. His fist connected with a jaw, and he dodged their punches and kicks, landing several of his own.

He let his anger fuel him. All he thought about was the fight.

And protecting Addie.

He'd never gotten the chance to defend his ma or Fiona.

His next punch broke the man's nose with a crunch. He heard Devyn scuffling with the final attacker.

Bram punched again. With a groan, the man collapsed on the dirty street. He gripped the front of the man's shirt and kept hitting him.

"He's out cold, Bram."

He ignored Devyn and kept hitting.

"Bram." She grabbed his bloody fist. "Addie will be worried."

He met her gaze, his blood still running hot.

Suddenly, a gun shot rang out. Years of experience had them both moving fast. He yanked her, spinning to cover her with his body.

A bullet whizzed past, and he shoved Devyn down beside his truck.

"Quit the hero bullshit, Bram." She shoved him and swiveled, her gun in hand.

"If you get hit, Killian will kill me. Better I take a bullet from a bad guy than my boss."

She rolled her eyes. "Where did the shot come from?"

"Don't know." Bram hunkered down and looked around. "But it's either Kozlov, or another friend of his."

A volley of bullets hit the side of his truck. They both ducked down and Bram drew his Glock out.

He tried to rise, but another bullet hit the side mirror of his truck and it exploded.

Fuck.

Devyn's gaze narrowed. "I'll crawl under the truck and—"

More gunfire. It was coming from the opposite direction.

"Two shooters." She cursed.

Dammit, they were pinned down. If they moved, they'd be taken out.

"We need a plan." She scanned the buildings around them.

More bullets hit, and this time, Bram saw a muzzle flash in a building nearby. "Brick building across the street. Third floor."

"I see him. Damn, if only I had a sniper rifle."

"If we cause a diversion, you can get into that building and take him out."

She shook her head. "Bram, we're pinned down."

The next volley had them dropping lower.

"The second shooter's moving closer," she said. "Where the hell did he go?"

Bram scanned the growing darkness. He lifted his Glock and waited.

Movement. A shadow.

A man rose from behind a car, his gun aimed at them. *Oh, fuck.*

A shot rang out, and the shooter jerked and dropped. *What the hell?*

Another man stalked down the center of the street, rifle held at his side.

Bram frowned.

Then the newcomer paused, lifted his rifle, and fired.

There was a short scream. Bram turned his head, just in time to see the shooter in the window tumble out and fall to the ground.

Devyn rose and dusted herself off. "Perfect timing as always, Shade."

Shade? Bram had only ever heard stories about the deep-cover CIA agent.

The man strode closer, swinging the rifle onto his broad shoulder.

He was tall, with wide shoulders, long legs, and dirty-blond hair that was currently pulled up in a small bun.

"I always like to save the day, Hellfire." His smile was wide and easy.

"So, you're Shade." Bram held out a hand.

The man smiled and shook. "You must be Excalibur."

"Bram O'Donovan."

"Cain."

Bram noted the agent didn't give his surname.

Shade turned to Devyn. "Hello, Mrs. Hawke." He shook his head. "I can't believe you married Steel."

"Sometimes I can't either, but I have zero regrets." Devyn hugged her former workmate and friend.

The spy tried to hide a wince.

She pulled back and frowned at him. "You're still hurt."

Shade had recently been attacked by a rogue agent, out to make a name for himself as an assassin of spies.

"I'm fine."

Devyn poked his side. Shade gritted his teeth.

"Broken ribs," she said. "You should be resting."

"I rested long enough. I wanted to check on you." He glanced at the bodies in the street. "I see it didn't take you long to find trouble."

"This is Bram's trouble. A Russian guy is stalking his woman. His *pregnant* woman."

Shade raised a brow and looked at the bodies. "He one of these?"

"No," Bram said. "These guys were doing him a favor."

Shade snorted. "I'm sure they regret it."

"We're still trying to find the asshole," Bram added.

"Well, one of these guys is still breathing." Shade smiled. "I suggest we take him in and ask him a few questions."

Devyn smiled back. "I knew I liked you."

"You have a funny way of showing it. You're usually cursing at me."

"Yes, well, you can be annoying. Bram here is my new bestie. You've been demoted."

Shade shook his head, then met Bram's gaze. They shared a look.

"Good luck with that," Shade said.

She elbowed him.

Then Bram headed toward the Russian thug who was groaning quietly on the ground.

He had questions, and he needed answers.

"JUST SIT DOWN THERE."

Addie let Hex push her into a chair near the office kitchen. There was a lush, green wall, and she'd ordinarily be soaking in all the plants, but she was too worried.

Hex had told her that Bram and Devyn had been attacked.

"Here, drink this." Hex shoved a mug into her hand.

Warmth seeped into Addie's cold fingers.

"It's tea," Hex said.

"They were attacked. Outnumbered."

"*Pfft*. Six against Bram and Devyn is not outnumbered." Hex tossed her pink-streaked hair back, and rested a hand on her hip. Today, she wore slim black pants and a high-necked, sleeveless shirt. "They weren't hurt. They'll be here soon."

"Where the hell are they?" Killian prowled in. He seemed his usual, cool self, until you looked at his eyes.

He was worried.

God, this scary man really loved his new wife.

Hex huffed out a breath. "They're *fine*. No one's hurt." She smiled. "And they said they had a prisoner."

Nick followed Killian in. "Apartment was empty. Kozlov's sleeping and eating there, but nothing else."

Addie sipped her tea, trying to keep her hand from

shaking. When would this Kozlov stop? She'd thought it was only him they had to deal with, but it seemed he had friends.

God, if something had happened to Bram and Devyn...

Her stomach twisted into a big knot. Maybe she should run? Get far away where Kozlov couldn't find her.

She pressed a hand to her belly. Where would she go? There was nowhere she could go.

Voices echoed from down the hall.

Devyn strode in like she didn't have a care in the world, Bram right behind her.

Addie drank in the sight of him. He was his usual scowling self. He looked fine, but his red hair was ruffled, and as she looked closer, she saw flecks of blood on his shirt.

Killian went straight to Devyn. "You're all right?" He cupped her jaw.

"Yes, Hawke. We kicked ass."

He hauled her in and kissed her. Addie's heart did a little sigh. Their love was obvious, and they looked really gorgeous together.

Bram knelt in front of Addie. She cupped his cheek, her stupid emotions welling up. "You're sure you're okay?"

He nodded.

She stroked his stubbled jaw. That's when she saw his knuckles were torn up and bloody. "Bram." She gripped his wrist.

"It's nothing. I promise."

Another tall man strode in, shoving a handcuffed

man ahead of him. The bound man looked blank faced, and surly.

His captor... Addie blinked. *Wow*. He looked like an action hero. He was tall, with broad shoulders that narrowed down to lean hips. A tight, gray Henley clung to his muscular chest, and his long legs were encased in black cargo pants. He had tawny-brown hair streaked with gold, and it was pulled up in a sexy man bun, that showcased his long face and strong jaw.

Then the man lifted his head, his gaze locking on Hex.

Hex stared back at him, appearing, for once, speechless.

"I brought you a gift, Steel," the newcomer drawled, amusement in his deep voice.

"Shade," Killian said. "Good to see you."

"We had a little help in our fight," Devyn said. "Shade is the king of popping up at the right time."

The man called Shade smiled across the room. "Hex, sneaky hacker goddess, we finally meet in person."

Hex sniffed. "I thought you'd be taller."

Addie choked back a laugh. The man was at least six-foot-three. She watched the way the two stared at each other, and suddenly, the room's temperature seemed to shoot up ten degrees. Interesting.

The handcuffed man made a sound and Shade pulled his gaze off Hex. His expression morphed into something scary. He shoved the man. "Talk."

Devyn circled in front of the prisoner, Killian beside her.

Now the temperature in the room felt like it dropped a few degrees.

"You know who I am?" Killian asked.

The man swallowed. "*Da.*"

"And yet, you still attacked my employee," Killian said in a silky voice. He glanced at Devyn, and his voice lowered more. "And my wife."

"Wife?" The man's voice cracked. "We didn't know! My boss, Nikitin, owed Kozlov a few favors. But the asshole clearly left out some details. Nikitin would *never* cause trouble with you."

Killian was silent for a moment. "Luckily, she can take care of herself."

The Russian swallowed and flicked a glance at Devyn. "Yeah."

"Where's Kozlov now?" Killian asked.

"I don't know! He's crazy. He's obsessed with some woman. He used to be solid, steady. A good enforcer. But now all he can talk about is the blonde." The man flicked a glance at Addie.

Bram put a hand on her shoulder. "Don't look at her."

The man jerked his gaze away.

Killian slid his hands in his pockets. Such an ordinary move, but it felt filled with menace.

"You go back to Nikitin, and you tell him that in order to make things right with me, I want to know where Kozlov is, or I want him delivered to me. This woman is under my protection. Her man is eager to make sure Kozlov stops tormenting her and leaves her alone."

Devyn shifted. "Do as he says, or you'll regret it."

The man on his knees swallowed.

Killian smiled. "My wife likes a good fight." He slid an arm around her. "Now, time for you to go."

Shade yanked the man to his feet and unfastened the handcuffs.

"You staying?" Killian asked Shade.

The man glanced at Hex. "Yeah, I'm not on anything right now. I think I might enjoy New York's charms." Shade dragged the man out.

Bram pulled Addie to her feet. "You need some rest."

"Especially with twins on board," Hex added.

Killian's brows rose. "Twins?"

Exclamations filled the room. Suddenly, Bram and Addie were surrounded by well-wishers. Addie smiled.

"Okay, enough. She needs to rest." Bram scooped her off her feet and headed for the elevator.

"I can walk, Bram."

"I don't care. You just tell me what you need and I'll give it to you."

She bit her lip. *You.* I need you. "You're the one who was in a gunfight. I should be looking after you."

"I always look after myself." He stepped into the elevator.

And that was the problem. He didn't expect anyone to look after him. He hadn't had that for a long time. Well, she was going to look after him.

"I know what I want," she said.

He met her gaze. "Anything."

CHAPTER TWELVE

Getting out of the shower, Bram swiped the towel over his wet skin and scowled at his reflection in the mirror.

There were quite a few scars on his chest—some from his military days, some still pink and healing from San Francisco.

He was a big brute. He didn't belong anywhere near Adaline Harris. He heard her singing through the door, out in the kitchen. She was cooking.

That's what she'd wanted to do, cook him dinner.

She was pregnant, with not one, but two babies, and he wanted her to rest and relax.

With a sigh, he headed for his closet. He knew he didn't have the ability to say no to her. And Addie wasn't stupid, so he was pretty sure she knew that. He pulled on jeans and a T-shirt.

As he reached the kitchen, amazing smells hit him.

Addie was stirring something on the stove. The table

was set, and candles were burning in the center. What the hell? He didn't own candles.

"Smells good," he said.

She squeaked and whirled. "For a big man, you move very quietly." Then she just stared at him.

He frowned, looking down. His jeans were old and faded at the stress points, and his T-shirt was just plain black. "What's wrong?"

"I..." She shook her head. "I've never seen you in jeans before. Or a T-shirt that hugs all your muscles."

It was true. He'd always come to her straight from work and had been wearing a suit.

"I mean, you look fine in a suit." She fiddled with her hair. "Like really great in a suit, but this works well, too. Really well."

He felt very uncharacteristic heat filling his cheeks. He cleared his throat. "Where did you get the candles?"

"Oh, Hex. She and Lainie, Nick's fiancée, dropped them off. Lainie seems really nice. I can't believe she's a hot shot CEO. They also left this—" with a flourish, Addie lifted a bottle of amber fluid off the counter.

It was a bottle of Redbreast 15-year-old. His favorite Irish whiskey.

"Have some." She beamed at him as she filled a glass with ice. "Do you put anything with it? Coke? Water?"

"No."

She poured it into the glass. "Lainie mentioned you've drunk Nick under the table several times." She handed him the glass.

He took it. "Wolf is a lightweight."

With a smile, she watched him take a sip, then she hurried back to the stove. "The steaks are almost ready. Sorry they aren't cooked on the grill, but the griddle pan doesn't do a bad job. Thanks for getting the groceries. I haven't had steak in forever. I made my own lemon rice, and green beans with walnuts in them with a balsamic dressing. It's delicious."

He loved it when she chattered in that excited voice. "You like cooking."

"Yes. I never had a chance to do it growing up. My parents never had time to cook, so we usually fended for ourselves. Grilled cheese sandwiches, or mac and cheese. Then once I started dancing..." she shrugged. "Dancers stick to yoghurt, fruit, and salads." She pulled out some plates. "You have a great kitchen, but you don't cook much. Half the cupboards are empty."

He shook his head.

"Okay." She waved at the table. "Take a seat. I'm serving up."

Bram found himself eating delicious steak, sipping excellent whiskey, and watching the candlelight flicker over Addie's pretty face.

"So, Shade seems interesting," she said.

"He's a deep-cover spy for the CIA. You can't tell anyone about him."

"I won't say a word. He somehow manages to come across both charming and dangerous. I'm glad he's on the side of the good guys."

"Me, too." No one would ever describe Bram as charming. He fought back a scowl.

"I'm really glad he helped you and Devyn."

Bram reached out and took her hand. "We would've been fine."

She set her fork down. "Nick said they didn't find anything at Kozlov's apartment. What about the storage place? Did you find anything?"

Feck. He didn't want to lie to her. "Not much. Kozlov wasn't there."

Her mouth flattened. "I can tell you're holding back."

"Addie—"

"I'm not weak or delicate, Bram."

"I know that, but I want to protect you."

"The best way to do that is keep me informed, not in the dark."

He sighed. "Photos. He had hundreds of photos of you."

"Oh." Dismay flowed over her face, then she lifted her chin. "We knew he was following me. It's not a surprise."

Bram tightened his grip, and stroked the pulse in her wrist. "He won't lay one hand on you."

"I know that." She cocked her head. "But you don't seem to trust that. Something is making you worried that you can't protect me."

A muscle ticked beside his eye.

"I trust you," she said quietly.

Shit, that hit him hard.

"But you don't trust yourself," she continued. "You won't let yourself open up fully with me. Why?"

Bram felt things shifting around inside him. Only Addie could do this to him. "Because I couldn't save my ma. Couldn't save my sister."

Addie watched him carefully. "Tell me how they were killed, Bram."

He closed his eyes. Old horrors were the worst. The edges were dulled and rusted, but they still cut far worse.

Slim fingers entwined with his. Just that small movement, joining them, knowing she was with him, was enough.

"We'd been to Dublin for the day. Ma took Fiona and me." It'd been a fun day, even with the dreaded shoe shopping. "I was in my last year of school, and still deciding what to do with my life." He'd also been fighting with his dad, who wanted him to go to work at the local mine. Bram hadn't known what he'd wanted, but he knew he didn't want to be stuck in a small village, doing the same things over and over again. "It was getting dark, and the car broke down."

Addie squeezed his fingers. "If it hurts too much, you don't have to tell me."

"No secrets." He wanted nothing between them. He took a deep breath. "A car stopped. Three men got out. They'd been drinking."

He saw her cheeks pale, but her gaze stayed locked on his. Yes, his Addie had steel under the sweet.

"They weren't interested in helping. I fought them, but they beat me up, and knocked me out. They shoved me in the back of our car. I came to in time to see them manhandling Ma and Fiona into their vehicle. I screamed, I chased them."

"Even though you were hurt."

He'd had a broken nose, a fractured collarbone, and a broken arm.

"Fiona screamed for me, but I couldn't help her." A ragged breath. "Two days later, the police found them in shallow graves. They'd been raped and strangled."

"Oh, Bram." Addie rose, bumping the table in her haste to get to him. He pulled her close, his face pressed to her belly. Her hands slid into his hair.

"I failed them," he whispered.

"No." Her hands tightened. "I'm so sorry. What happened, it's evil, but it wasn't your fault. Were the men caught?"

"Yes."

The men had gone to jail. All three had been killed behind bars in jailhouse attacks. Bram had made sure of it.

"It was *not* your fault. I know it's horrible to be help-less, but you were a boy on the verge of manhood, against three grown men." She smoothed his hair. "Your mother and sister would not want you blaming yourself."

He looked up at her. "If anyone touches you, takes you from me..."

"Then I'll know you're coming for me." She cupped his cheek. "I'll know."

He shuddered. Her trust was such a precious thing.

Then she gasped.

"Addie?" His pulse leaped.

"The babies." She pressed his hand over her belly. "One of them is kicking."

He felt the tiny flutter under his palm. Pure wonder filled him, and Addie beamed at him.

"I felt these little pops the other day, but I wasn't sure."

"That's definitely a kick." He caressed her bump, amazed. Protectiveness filled him. "I'll do anything for you."

Her face turned serious. "I know, but I also want you to do things for yourself, Bram. Stop punishing yourself."

"Giving you what you want and need, that makes me happy."

Something worked behind her eyes. "Anything?"

His hands tightened on her. "Anything."

"Okay." She licked her lips and stepped back. "I want you to take all your clothes off."

ADDIE'S BELLY was fluttering and her cheeks were flushed.

Bram was frozen, staring at her.

Be brave. This is your man. Show him. Give him what he needs.

"Addie—"

She shook her head. "No. You said you'd give me what I want. What I need. I need you naked so I can touch you." She took a step toward the living area. "Let's move to the couch."

She walked over, trying to feel sensual. She felt his gaze on her—hot and hungry. Or at least she hoped it was. She wanted him to look at her the way he'd looked at her on those hot nights in her old apartment.

Like he could hardly believe she was real.

She sank onto the tan leather, sinking back against the cushions. He took a second, but slowly followed.

"Addie," he tried again.

"I want you, Bram. *You.* Your big, strong body, your tough protectiveness, your sometimes-surly personality."

His scowl deepened.

She smiled. "I like everything about you, just as you are."

Green eyes flicked up to her, almost startled. Had no one ever told him that before?

She nodded her head. "Clothes off, please."

He was still for a second, then he gripped the back of his T-shirt and pulled it over his head.

Oh. That broad chest, the slabs of muscle, the dusting of red hair. She never got tired of looking at him. She felt a pulse between her legs, a damp rush of heat.

And a sense of power.

This man—this strong protector—was like a knight, ready to do her bidding.

"The rest of your clothes, Bram."

His face was unreadable, but his fingers went to the button and zipper on his jeans. She licked her lips.

Then he shucked his jeans and black boxer shorts off.

God. Everything about him was perfect to her. Hard abs, thick powerful thighs, thick cock weeping for her.

"You're so beautiful," she murmured.

He snorted. "Hardly. You're beautiful."

"Well, you're beautiful to me." She crooked her finger.

He moved closer until he stood right in front of her. She skimmed her hands up his stomach, felt his muscles flex.

"I need you, Bram. You're the thing I need most of all."

He reached out, fingers skimming her jaw and sliding into her hair, tugging it free of her hair tie. "I was yours a long time ago, sunshine. I just couldn't find the words to tell you."

Addie smiled, warmth unfurling inside her. Then it stuttered. "You're not with me just because I'm pregnant?"

His hand tightened. "I was already looking for you. About to unleash everything I had to find you."

She circled his cock with her hand, and he groaned.

Knowing that just a small touch from her could affect this man like this made her shiver. "I'm going to suck your cock now."

He groaned.

"And..." Being bold wasn't easy for her, but the way Bram watched her, he made her feel safe. "Then I want your mouth on me."

His eyes flashed. "Between your legs? On your sweet pussy?"

"*Yes.*" Her other hand clenched on the leather. "But first I want you to touch yourself."

His hand closed over hers and they stroked him together. They pumped his big cock and Bram groaned.

"Fuuuck."

She pressed one hand to his muscular thigh and leaned in. She loved the feel of his cock, hard and soft at the same time.

A little like Bram himself. He tried not to show a soft side, but she knew it was there.

"Mine." She'd never claimed anything or anyone in her entire life. Never trusted anything would actually be hers.

He didn't get a chance to respond because she leaned forward, and licked the head of his cock.

He groaned, and the salty taste of him made her moan. Desire pushed her hard, and she sucked him deep, trying to take as much of him in as she could.

With a curse, his hips thrust forward.

Addie felt the head of his cock hit the back of her throat. Her eyes watered and she swallowed.

"Dammit, I'm sorry." His voice was harsh as he started to pull back.

She gripped his hips and held him in place. She sucked harder, bobbing her head. She wasn't very experienced, but she loved the sounds he made.

"*Addie*." With a growl, he pulled free of her mouth.

Seconds later, Bram pushed her onto her back. He loomed over her, a feral look on his face.

Oh. Her belly clenched. He looked like a warrior pushed too far.

He stripped her clothes off, and pushed her thighs apart. Then his mouth was on her.

With a sharp cry, she arched up to his mouth. He devoured her. Stubble scraped her sensitive skin, his tongue lapped at her before he sucked on her clit. She moaned desperately.

"You even taste like sunshine. My sweet Addie."

Her fingers tangled in his hair. "I *need* you." She was so close, but she wanted to come with him inside her. Joined to him. "I need you inside me."

With a raw sound, he sat back. Her belly clenched even tighter. What a picture he made, naked on the couch—all tense muscles and flushed skin.

"Come here," he growled.

She sat up a little more, moving a little awkwardly thanks to her belly, but finally she straddled him.

His hands clenched on her hips, his gaze locked on her face.

"I ache, Bram. For you." She kissed him and lowered her hips.

His cock brushed against her clit, and she whimpered. He deepened the kiss. She felt his cock push inside her, just the head. She loved the delicious stretch.

His big hands slid down and clenched on her ass. She saw his jaw flex.

"Don't hold back," she ordered.

"I don't want to hurt you."

"You'll only hurt me if you don't give me all of you." She bit his bottom lip. "*Please.*"

He groaned her name and thrust his hips up.

She cried out. She was full of him. He caught her cry, urging her to move. She started to ride him, impaling herself on his thick cock. It felt like the first time all over again.

"That's it, sunshine. Take it. Take me."

She gripped his broad shoulders and looked into his eyes. Then she felt his thumb at her clit. "Bram."

She'd never allowed anyone this close. Close enough to see inside her—to her most vulnerable parts. The parts she worried no one would love. The parts no one had ever loved.

"I've got you, Addie. Always. Give yourself to me. I want you. *Always*."

As he kissed her again, her climax exploded. Sensation poured through her.

"Bram, come with me!"

He groaned, his fingers sinking into the flesh of her buttocks. As she drowned in the searing emotions, she felt Bram's big body tense beneath her.

He gave a low roar as he spilled inside her. "My Addie."

She clung to him as he pulled her closer and buried his face in her hair.

"Don't let go," she whispered.

"Never."

CHAPTER THIRTEEN

Bram carried Addie to the bedroom. She snuggled into him, and he felt her lips at his neck.

He lay her down gently and climbed on the bed beside her.

She cuddled against his chest, one leg pressed over his, and he felt her baby belly press to his side.

She played with his nipple. "That was amazing."

"I love touching you."

She went silent, not meeting his gaze.

"Addie?"

Her gaze flicked up. "I wasn't sure if you were just taking care of me because of the babies."

His hand tightened on her. "Never doubt how much I want you, Addie. There isn't a fucking minute of the day that I'm not thinking about you."

She let out a happy sigh. "No one's ever wanted me like you do."

He was pretty fucking happy about that. The men around her were eejits, but that meant he had Addie all to himself. He still wasn't sure he was good enough for her...

"You could do better, Addie. I'm too old, too rough, too—"

"Stop it." She frowned. "You're ten years older than me, Bram. There are people with larger age gaps than that. I told you. I like you just the way you are." She wriggled against him, and he felt the hot core of her against his thigh—still slick from them both.

Her words burrowed into his chest, but the feel of her short-circuited all his thoughts. "What do you need, Addie?" He stroked her ass cheek.

"It's the pregnancy hormones. And you. I'm always thinking about you."

His blood fired. "Not as much as I think about you." He rolled her over and his gaze dropped to her pretty breasts. They were much larger than normal.

He propped her up on the pillows, and cupped the curve of one breast. She made a husky sound. He played with the nipple, then lowered his head. He lapped, then sucked. She writhed, and he moved to the other nipple.

"Oh, God. They're so sensitive." Her head thrashed on the pillow.

He was hard again, his cock throbbing. He pushed her breasts together, kneaded them gently.

"These were pretty before, and are just as pretty now." He ran his thumb over her nipple.

She pressed her hands over his. "Come up here."

His gut clenched. "What?"

"Up here, Bram. Now." There was a bossy note to her voice.

He pinched one nipple. "You like knowing I'd do anything for you."

"Yes." Her blue eyes were hazy with desire.

He straddled her torso carefully, not putting any weight on her.

She guided his rock-hard cock between her plump breasts.

"*Fuck*," he groaned.

"Bram," she breathed.

He thrust against the soft flesh as she pushed her breasts together. Her skin was flushed, her lips open as she watched him.

"I love how big and strong you are," she said.

Damn. He wouldn't last long. If he wasn't careful, he'd spill all over her chest. He shifted off her, ignoring her protests and knelt between her legs. He slid his hands under her ass and lifted her.

Shit, just looking at her had him ready to blow.

He guided his cock to her and slid it through her pretty folds.

She moaned. "Don't tease me."

He stroked again. "I think you like it when I tease you."

She arched up. "*Bram*."

"Right here, sunshine. I'll give you everything you need. I'll work every day to prove I deserve you." He pushed forward, his cock sliding into her tight warmth. Desire ran through him like electricity. "You feel so good, Addie." He rocked his hips forward. "I can't be gentle."

"I don't need gentle." Her hands clenched on his

biceps, nails biting into his skin. "I just need you. All of you."

He yanked her body closer and thrust deep. So deep. Her sweet cries were music to his ears. He pumped into her—harder, faster. Perspiration coated his skin.

"You mine, Addie Harris?"

"Yes. *Yours.*"

He planted his fists in the bed either side of her. "Mine. My babies in your belly. My cock inside you. My bed you sleep in."

"Bram!" Then she was coming.

He'd never seen anything prettier. Hot pressure coiled at the base of his spine, heat sizzling through him. Her pussy clenched hard on his cock, and he couldn't hold back.

With a low groan, he thrust deep, and emptied himself inside her.

It felt like everything was ripped out of him. Everything he had was now hers—his come, his heart, his body, his soul.

Bram collapsed on the bed beside her and pulled her close.

She nuzzled into him, her body limp. "I like bossing you around."

He chuckled. "I could tell."

She lifted her head, wonder in her eyes. "You laughed."

"I do. Sometimes."

"Not enough." She pressed a kiss to his chest. "I'm going to make you laugh more, Bram O'Donovan. I'm going to do everything I can to make you happy."

His heart squeezed. Addie was like a drug, and he was addicted. She'd ruined him. She'd dragged him out of the shadows and into the sunshine. She'd definitely ruined him for anyone else. The thought of touching any other woman but Addie left him queasy.

But first and foremost, he had to find and stop Kozlov.

Bram would do anything to keep her and the babies safe. *I'm coming for you, asshole.*

"Bram?"

"Mmm?"

She lifted her head, a wide smile on her face. "I have a few other things I need you to do for me."

His blood heated. "Whatever you need, sunshine."

"I'M FINE, Saskia. Everything's...well great, considering."

"You have a *stalker*, Addie," her friend said across the phone line. "And you didn't tell me."

Addie paced across the command center. "I know. I'm sorry. I didn't want you to worry, and I'm just used to depending on myself. I'm trying to get used to accepting help."

"Good. You should. Well, I am glad I was wrong about Bram."

Addie smiled. Memories of the night before flitting through her head. "Me too. He's been so good. So protective."

"So, he's taking good care of you?"

"Oh, definitely. He's so sweet."

Saskia snorted. "That's not a word I've ever used to describe Bram O'Donovan."

"He's gruff on the outside, but with me..."

"He's sweet."

"Yes. I'm in love with him, Saskia."

"Oh, Addie, I can hear that in your voice. And how does he feel?"

She bit her lip. "He's not much of a talker, especially about feelings."

Did he love her? Could he ever feel that for her? Sometimes when he looked at her, there was so much in his gaze.

"That's an understatement." Saskia sounded amused.

"Saskia, there's something else. Don't be mad."

"Girl, you have to get better at sharing."

"Okay. Um...I'm pregnant. Bram is the father."

"What?" Saskia screeched. "You were alone, scared, and stressed, and you didn't tell me you were pregnant? God, you got a job at a bar, Addie."

"You'd just fallen in love, and were making a life with Cam in San Francisco. I wasn't going to dump my problems on you. How is Cam by the way?"

"He's fine. *Very* fine, and do not change the subject. Pregnant. Are you all right? Healthy? Feeling okay?"

"I feel great, especially now."

"I can't believe you didn't tell me."

"We just had the ultrasound. Bram looked like he preferred to be heading to war. And we found out we're having twins. A boy and a girl."

Another squeal across the line. Addie smiled. It was nice to have people excited for her, unlike her mom.

"You have to rest and take good care of yourself," Saskia said.

"I will." Addie sat down, and saw Hex hunched over the computer, lost in her work. Addie knew that Hex was doing everything she could to search for Kozlov.

Addie's stomach curdled. Bram, Killian, and the others were out talking to contacts, and searching the streets.

She wanted this to be over. She wanted to get on with her life.

"Congratulations, Addie," Saskia said. "Bram will take care of you. All three of you. I'm so mad to hear that this asshole stalker and that woman in the Sentinel Security office kept you two apart."

"It all worked out in the end."

"And my brother dealt with Pam. And Bram, Killian, and the team will stop this Kozlov."

Addie rubbed her belly. "He worked for Mikhailov."

"I heard. I'm so sorry you ever got dragged into this."

"It's not your fault, Saskia. You were a victim, too."

"I know, but a part of me is kind of glad I got Cam out of the whole ordeal." There was a dreamy sound to her voice.

Saskia totally loved Camden Morgan, who worked for Norcross Security.

"How's your ballet school coming along?" Addie asked.

"So great! I've found the perfect space. It's going to be amazing." Excitement filled her voice.

"You won't miss the stage?"

"No. I was ready for a change. Cam and the school, they've become more important to me." She paused. "You're worried about your dancing?"

"Actually...no. I don't think I want to go back to it." It felt good to say the words out loud. "I just don't want to be a failure."

"Addie, goals change. That's allowed."

"I know. But I left my hometown, determined to make it as a dancer." Addie's gaze turned inward. "I've been focused on that, struggled for it, for so long."

"You have to do what makes you happy, and not worry about what other people think."

"I don't want to go back on the stage, but I don't want to give up dancing completely."

"There are other ways to keep dance in your life. Look at me."

"Well, I think I'm going to be pretty busy for the foreseeable future," Addie said.

"You think?" Saskia laughed.

"But I'm going to think about what I want to do." She felt like a balloon was filling in her chest. The future yawned ahead, filled with opportunity. It felt good.

All except the fact that Kozlov was out there, wanting to steal her future from her.

But you aren't alone, Addie. It's going to be all right.

"OKAY, TAKE CARE OF YOURSELF, ADDIE," Saskia said. "I'm going to plan a trip over to give you a baby shower."

"Oh, that sounds amazing." Addie's chest warmed.

"We'll talk soon. Stay close to Bram."

Addie laughed. "I am."

"Mmm, I'm sure all that gruff dedication pays off when it's focused on you."

She blushed. "Saskia..."

"Take care."

Addie slipped her phone into her pocket, but the warm glow faded. Ilya Kozlov was still out there. Hunting her.

"Hex, any updates?"

The tech guru lifted her head and blinked. "Nothing yet. No sign of the fucker."

"Are Bram and the others okay?"

"Yes. Bram was extra scowly earlier, but then I swear I saw him smile."

Addie hid her own smile.

"He wants you and the babies safe," Hex said.

"I want that, too."

"So, I see stubble burn on your neck, and a dreamy look in your eyes. You successfully seduced your grumpy baby daddy."

Addie couldn't stop a grin. "Maybe."

Hex rolled her eyes and smiled. "I'm happy for you."

"I'm in love with him."

"Ah, if you thought that was a secret, I hate to tell you, but you were doing a bad job of hiding it."

Addie nibbled her lip. "He hasn't said it. I have no idea how he truly feels."

"Give him time. You make him happy. And if any man deserves that, it's Bram."

Addie thought of everything he'd told her about his mother and sister. She was going to make him happy. She rubbed her belly. Her and their babies.

Hex's computer pinged and she whirled.

"What is it?" Addie asked.

"Facial recognition got a hit." The hacker frowned. "It's only a partial match. It can't be right. It's from a traffic camera in Georgia."

"Georgia?" Her pulse leaped. "Maybe he's heading south? Maybe he's given up?"

"As much as I might want to believe it, I don't think Bram will trust it. Not until he has Kozlov for himself."

"So maybe this image isn't Kozlov?" Addie asked.

Hex tapped and the image appeared on the screen. It showed a man in profile, sitting in the driver's seat of a truck with a ball cap pulled low. It was hard to tell.

"Maybe," Hex said.

Addie's phone started vibrating and she pulled it out. The display read, *Mom*. Her belly clenched. Her mother hadn't been nice or understanding about the pregnancy. Addie wasn't sure she wanted to deal with more of that right now.

But she sighed and answered.

"Hi, Mom."

"Adaline."

The terror in her mother's voice froze her. "Mom?"

"He's going to kill us, Addie." Her mother's harsh breathing filled the line. "He's tied us up. He beat your father."

God. Addie's heart stopped. Kozlov had her parents.

"He said he'll kill us. You have to come, alone, or we're dead."

"Mom, stay calm. You're at home?"

"Yes, Adaline, and he's not joking. He's—"

The line went dead.

God, she sucked in a shuddering breath and lifted her head.

"Addie, what's wrong?" Hex asked.

"Call Bram. Kozlov has my parents."

CHAPTER FOURTEEN

As soon as Bram stalked into the command center, Addie raced over to him.

He hugged her tightly.

"Bram." She was fighting back tears. "Kozlov has my parents."

He hugged her harder. "I'll fix this."

"My parents...they aren't perfect, but they aren't bad. I love them. I don't want them hurt."

"We're going to save them." And he'd finally take down this fucker Kozlov in the process.

Bram looked at Killian.

"The jet is being fueled," Killian said. "We can be there in a few hours."

"I'll have SUVs waiting for you when you land." Hex spun. "Addie's parents' place is on the outskirts of a small town called—"

"Hickory Ridge," Addie said.

Hex nodded. "To get eyes and ears, we'll need a drone in the air. I'm coming."

"I'm coming, too." Shade pushed away from the wall where he'd been standing.

Devyn nodded. "With me, Killian, Bram, Matteo, and Nick, plus Shade, we can easily neutralize this guy."

"Hadley is going to be mad she missed out on the action," Hex said.

Devyn looked at Addie. "I promise we'll do everything we can to get your parents out safely."

"Let's get to the airport," Killian ordered. "Grab whatever gear you need."

Hex whirled, snatching up a padded case and setting it on the desk. When she opened it, Bram saw the high-tech drone nestled inside.

"I'm coming too," Addie said.

"What?" Bram spun and resisted the urge to shake her. "No. It's too dangerous."

"He's after *me*." Her face was set in serious lines. "You might need me to talk to him, or lure him out—"

"*No.*"

She straightened. "Bram, we have no idea what will happen. These are my *parents*. It's because of me that they're in danger."

He pressed a palm to her belly. "You have other lives to protect."

Her face softened. "I know. I'm not suggesting I charge into the fight, but I need to come."

He looked at the floor, gut churning. He wanted her safe, and very, very far away from Ilya Kozlov. Several states away worked for him.

She pressed her palms to his chest. "Bram."

Fuck. He couldn't say no. And she was right, they might need her. "You'll stay on the jet."

She nodded. "Absolutely."

"You're not going *anywhere* near Kozlov."

"I won't."

Bram pulled her in for a hard kiss, then pressed her to his chest. Her arms wrapped around him, and they held each other tight. "I'll get your parents out."

"I know," she murmured. "I trust you. But be careful, Bram. All of you." She met his gaze. "You come back to me. To us." She touched her belly.

Throat tight, he nodded.

"Let's move," Killian said.

The room exploded in a rush of activity. All the Sentinel Security team knew how to prepare for missions. They'd done it too many times to count. Hex packed her electronic gear while the rest of them loaded duffel bags with weapons, vests, and gear.

Soon, the convoy of SUVs was headed to Teterboro airport. When they pulled in, the Sentinel Security jet sat on the tarmac, its pilot, Ric, doing the last-minute flight checks.

"Nice wings, Steel," Shade said.

"If you want a job, I'll give you one." Killian inclined his head at the aircraft. "You can fly in her whenever you need."

Bram saw Hex pull a face.

Shade just smiled at Killian. "Not quite ready to give up working for Uncle Sam yet."

Bram got Addie settled on the jet.

"It's so fancy." She stroked the cream-leather seat.

There was a small, well-stocked galley kitchen, lots of wide armchairs, and touches of glossy wood.

"Addie, I need you to draw up the floor plan of the inside of your parents' house." Hex dropped down in the seat across from them with a notepad. "We need to plan."

Most of the flight was spent going over the plan to infiltrate Addie's childhood home and rescue her parents.

Bram looked down at a map of Hickory Ridge, noting the location of the house, just out of town.

Kozlov was getting desperate. How far would he go to get to Addie? And what would he do once he realized that she'd never be his?

Bram remembered his helplessness as his mother and Fiona were dragged away from him. He couldn't stand for the same thing to happen with Addie.

"Bram?"

He looked up and met Killian's gaze.

"You're not alone. We're all in this." Killian gripped Bram's shoulder. "We'll get Addie's parents back, and keep her safe. We're with you, every step of the way."

The tightness in Bram's chest eased. "Thanks, Killian."

The other man nodded. "You don't need to thank me."

Devyn dropped down beside Bram and gave him a nudge. "We've got this, bestie."

Bram nodded. But he knew he wouldn't breathe easy until Kozlov was out of action, and Bram finally had Addie safely back in New York.

The jet landed at a private airstrip. The strip was

surrounded by trees, and not much else. Three black SUVs were waiting for them.

Hex lifted her gear and headed for the lead vehicle.

Shade followed her down the steps, frowning at her. "Aren't you staying with the jet?"

"No," she said tartly. "I need to get the drone in the air, and I need to be close to it."

Shade crossed his arms. "It's too dangerous."

She bared her teeth. "I'll be staying in the car, James Bond. And if Kozlov comes too close—" she smiled "—I can take care of myself."

"Everyone load up." Killian was wearing black cargo pants and a bulletproof tactical vest. They'd all changed on the jet. He gave Addie a nod and headed to the SUVs.

Bram went to Addie. She sat in the large seat on the jet, twisting her hands in her lap. "Bram..."

He leaned down and kissed her. "It's going to be fine."

She nodded, but worry lined her face. He knelt down and pressed a kiss to her belly. She cupped his head.

Then he rose and looked at Ric. The pilot stood in the cockpit doorway.

"I'll take care of her," the pilot said. "Maybe we'll play cards. Ever play poker, Addie?"

"No."

"I'll teach you." The pilot gave Bram a nod.

He nodded back and headed for the stairs.

"Bram." She ran down the aisle to him and leaped. He caught her and she kissed him, a little wild, a little desperate.

He took a few seconds to kiss her back, absorbing the

taste of her. "Addie, I'll get your parents safe." He slid his hand into her golden hair. "I'll make you safe. I'll always fight for you."

"I know." She gripped him harder. "I love you, Bram."

The words hit him like a blunt instrument. He just stared at her. No one had told him that they loved him since he'd lost his ma and Fiona.

Addie slid down until her feet touched the floor, and smiled at him.

He couldn't speak, couldn't get his brain functioning. *She loved him.*

"Bram," Nick barked from outside the jet. "Get your boots moving."

"Go," she said. "I'll see you when you get back."

Bram walked down the steps. *Addie loved him.*

He slid into the SUV. *Addie loved him.* Fuck, he loved her, too.

"You okay?" Nick asked.

"I'm in love with Addie."

"Wow, not too quick, are you, Excalibur?"

"Fuck you, Wolf."

Nick laughed. "Enjoy the ride man. The right woman is the best thing that'll ever happen to you."

As the convoy pulled out, Bram was smiling.

BRAM QUIETLY CREPT through the trees. The grass in the yard out the front of the small house was yellow and overgrown. It didn't appear that gardening was a high priority for Addie's parents.

The house was small and needed painting, but the tiny porch was swept clean, and a potted plant sat beside the door. An old truck was parked beside the building.

He didn't like that Addie's family had essentially left her all alone to fend for herself. It sounded like she'd been looking out for herself since she was a little girl. But he knew she cared for her parents, so he'd do his best to save them.

The air was still, no sound except the birds chirping in the trees.

"In position." Devyn's voice came through his earpiece. She was at the back of the house with Killian.

"In position." Nick and Matteo were on the western side.

Shade moved preternaturally quietly beside Bram.

Bram's gut was tight. He had a bad feeling. He kept trying to shake it off. The last time he'd felt like that, it had been on a mission that had blown up in his face.

And that long-ago night when his ma's car had broken down.

"No movement inside," Bram said.

"The drone is in position," Hex said.

Bram heard the faintest whirr as the drone passed overhead.

"Two heat signatures in the center of the living room," she said. "They're not moving."

That had to be Addie's parents. "Where's Kozlov?" Bram muttered.

"No sign of a third person," Hex said. "He has the skills to evade heat detection."

Bram still didn't like it.

"Bram and Shade, go through the front," Killian said. "Devyn and I are coming through the back. Wolf and Hades, watch the outside."

Bram moved forward, rifle in his hands. He'd keep his promise to Addie.

He reached the porch.

"Stop," Shade hissed.

Bram stilled.

The other man crouched, and pointed a finger at a wire crossing the steps. It was hard to see.

Shade followed it under the porch and his face hardened. "It's hooked to a grenade."

Fuck. He touched his ear. "Killian, Devyn. Watch out for booby-traps. The front step is wired." He carefully stepped over the wire, toward the door.

"Acknowledged," Killian replied. "Be careful. Hex, the instant this asshole pops up, tell us."

"On it, boss man."

Bram tried the front door handle, and it turned. He pulled back and checked for any tripwires. "Clear."

He nodded at Shade, and pointed, then he slid inside. Shade followed him.

An older couple were tied to chairs positioned in the center of the worn carpet. Their mouths were covered with duct tape. When they saw him, their eyes widened. He scanned the room, and checked behind the couches. Shade moved swiftly into the small kitchen.

"Clear," Shade called.

"We're coming in," Devyn said. "The back door was rigged with a booby trap as well." A second later, Devyn and Killian came through the kitchen, then moved to check the bedrooms.

The house wasn't big, and Bram imagined it had been a tight fit with five children.

"House is clear," Killian said. "Hex, any sign of Kozlov?"

"Negative, Killian."

Fucking fuck. Bram bit back his frustration. He moved to the Harrises.

Shirley Harris had faded blonde hair threaded with gray. She had it pulled back in a bun. Her face was lined, but he could see the good bone structure. Addie looked a lot like her mom. Harold Harris had a barrel-shaped body, and the florid look of someone who drank too much. His gray hair was thinning, there were fresh bruises on his jaw, and one eye was swollen closed. He'd taken a beating.

As gently as he could, Bram pulled the tape off Addie's mother. Shade did the same for her father. The man grunted and looked dazed.

Addie's mother gasped. "Oh my gosh."

"Are you all right?" Bram asked, as he started untying the ropes binding her to the chair.

"My husband..."

"We'll get you both to the hospital. Where's the man who did this?"

"He left," Mrs. Harris rubbed her wrists, her gaze narrowing on Bram. "Who are you?"

"I'm Addie's man. Bram O'Donovan."

"Her man?" The woman's eyebrows went up as she looked at him. "You're the father of her baby."

It was up to Addie to share the news on the twins. He nodded.

The woman got a pinched look on her face. "You left her."

"It was a misunderstanding. I'm never leaving her again."

The woman glanced at the others on the team.

"Mrs. Harris, Addie is mine." He waited until she looked back at him. "I will protect her and give her whatever she wants."

The older woman shook her head. "The girl was always dreaming. She wanted to dance. She wanted a man who'd love her."

"Dreams do come true sometimes. Now, Kozlov..."

"That's the bastard's name?" Mr. Harris said, voice wobbly.

Bram nodded. "He's obsessed with Addie."

Addie's mother shuddered. "He left about an hour ago."

"Nope, hour and a half," Mr. Harris said.

"It was an hour, Harold," she snapped. Then she met Bram's gaze. "He said he was going to get her, and that we'd never see her again."

A chill ran through Bram, and he straightened. "Hex, call Ric."

"Okay," Hex responded. "Hang on."

The others all tensed, watching and waiting.

"No answer," Hex said.

Bram pulled out his phone and pressed the button for Addie.

Her phone rang and rang.

Fuck.

He charged for the door. "Kozlov has Addie!"

ADDIE TRIED to play a few games on her phone, then she set it down with a huff. She'd played cards with Ric for a bit, but it was clear that she was terrible at it, and she couldn't focus.

She rose and paced the aisle of the jet.

She was too worried. About her parents. About the Sentinel Security team. About Bram.

"It will be over soon, babies." She rubbed circles on her stomach and felt a little kick. "Daddy will be back soon."

The image of Bram cradling a baby made her smile.

Ric was outside checking something on the plane. Maybe some fresh air would help her?

She carefully descended the stairs. "Ric?"

She didn't see him. She scanned the area around the landing strip, hoping to see the SUVs coming back. She wanted Bram's arms around her.

At the bottom of the stairs, she glanced toward the back of the jet. Her heart clenched. A body was lying on the ground, legs sticking out on the other side of the jet. Those were Ric's boots.

Her chest twisted. *Oh no.* Had he fallen?

"Ric!"

She'd taken one step when someone grabbed her in a firm grip from behind. She was whirled around.

She looked up into a hard face.

Kozlov. Her stomach turned over. *No.*

"What did you do to Ric?" She hated that her voice trembled.

"Ric can't help you." Her stalker smiled. "Hello, Adaline."

"Leave. Me. Alone." She tried to jerk away from him, and at the same time, she slipped her phone from her pocket. She knew he'd take it away from her if he saw it.

He pulled her closer, and she smelled sweat and cinnamon from the gum he chewed. The combination nearly made her gag.

"I can't leave you, because you're mine," he said, his accent thick.

"I'm *not.*" She tried to yank away, and pressed the screen of her phone. Then she dropped it in the grass.

He dragged her closer, hands rough, and she cried out.

"You're going to be my wife. I have a home all ready for us. It's waiting for you."

Horror spread through her. He was truly sick, living in some deluded fantasy. "I'll never marry you. I don't love you. I love somebody else."

"You'll forget him." Kozlov dragged her toward the trees. "Soon, you'll love only me."

Bram! Mentally, she cried out for him.

He'd come for her. No matter what. She knew her man would never give up.

She had to be strong and wait.

CHAPTER FIFTEEN

B efore the SUV had even stopped beside the jet, Bram shoved the door open.

As his feet skidded in the dirt, he paused, listening. Nothing but silence all around.

"Addie!" he roared.

No response.

"Shit, Ric." Devyn raced toward the fallen pilot. The man lay on the ground outside.

Bram jogged to the stairs.

"He's alive," Devyn yelled. "Looks like he took a blow to the head."

Bram thundered up the steps and ducked inside the aircraft, but he already knew.

It was empty.

He took in the empty chairs and checked the galley.

"*Fuck*." He kicked one of the seats. Addie was gone. Kozlov had her. His heartbeat pounded in his ears.

"Bram?" Killian said from the doorway.

"She's not here. He has her."

Bram shouldered past his boss and stomped off the jet. Nick and Matteo had taken Addie's parents to the local hospital, but Hex and Shade stood beside Devyn as the woman treated Ric. Hex had a heavy-duty tablet in her hand and looked distraught. Shade's face looked grim.

"This was all part of his plan." Bram pressed his hands to the back of his neck.

He couldn't lose it. He had to hold it together.

"We'll find her," Killian said, voice ringing like steel. "Hex?"

The hacker stepped forward, tapping on her tablet. "The security cameras on the jet were jammed." Worry lined her face. "We have no recording of what went on here."

"So, we have no idea what he's driving, or where he's heading." Bram had failed Addie. It was hard to breathe.

A ringing sound made his head jerk up. A cellphone?

They all turned. He strode toward the sound and saw Addie's phone resting in the grass. He snatched it up.

Had Kozlov tossed it here?

Bram saw her mother was trying to call her. He sucked in a breath. "The phone's recording."

Hex smiled. "That's our girl." She took the phone, tapped, then played the recording.

"Leave me alone." Addie's frightened voice.

Bram closed his eyes. She was trying so hard to be brave.

"I can't, because you're mine."

Fucking Kozlov.

"I'm *not*."

Bram listened to the replay. He heard his clever girl

drop the phone without Kozlov noticing. But the man didn't say where he was taking her.

"It doesn't help," Bram said.

"It might." Shade stepped forward, his hands in his pockets. "He says that he has a home set up. Waiting and ready. That takes time. Where's he been? Is this place in New York?"

Killian nodded slowly. "Maybe not. Where did Kozlov go after his employment with Mikhailov imploded? He didn't come straight to New York. There were several months before he started stalking Addie."

Bram had just figured the asshole was stewing on his obsession. Getting up the courage to act on it.

But maybe he'd been somewhere, putting a house together while his deluded fantasies grew.

"I'll start digging," Hex said.

"We all will," Killian said. "Let's tear his life apart. If you need hacking help..."

Hex nodded. "I'll contact Remi or Ace."

Remi was a former hacker who'd once worked for Sentinel Security, before she'd married tech billionaire Maverick Rivera. Ace Oliveira worked for Norcross Security in San Francisco. They'd both helped out Sentinel Security before.

"Hex, we also need a local base of operations," Devyn said. "Something close by."

Bram was glad they weren't heading back to New York. The thought of leaving without Addie ripped him apart.

"I'll find us somewhere," Hex said.

Devyn touched Bram's arm. "I won't tell you not to

worry, but we are going to find her. She's waiting for you. She's going to keep herself and those babies safe until you do."

Bram fought to get some air into his tight lungs. He imagined Addie smiling at him.

I trust you.

I know you'll come.

He wasn't helpless anymore. He wasn't a teenage boy watching his mother and sister ripped away from him.

This time, he'd find his woman and bring her home.

Hold on for me, Addie.

He didn't want to consider what she might need to do to survive. He gritted his teeth. He wasn't giving up. She wouldn't give up.

"Let's find my woman."

ADDIE GROANED, her eyelids fluttering. She felt so groggy.

Strong arms slid under her and lifted her.

"There you go, *milaya*."

The male voice had a strong accent, but it wasn't Irish.

She opened her eyes, light stabbing at her like needles. She moaned. She was being lifted out of a car.

Everything whirled sickeningly.

She whimpered. It felt familiar. For a second, she was plunged back into her nightmare abduction. She'd been drugged then, too, woozy, carted around.

No, Mikhailov was gone.

She turned her head and saw Kozlov.

No. She moaned again.

"Shh, sweet Adaline."

"You...drugged me."

"Just so you'd sleep."

"Babies..." Worry spiked through her.

"I checked. I used a drug that won't hurt you." He shot a sour look at her stomach. "Or them."

Bram would lose his mind when he found her gone. When he learned Kozlov had her, he'd blame himself. He'd relive his own nightmare of losing his mother and sister.

Addie managed to drag in a deep breath. She had to stay strong—for Bram, for their babies.

"Ric. The pilot. Did you—?"

"He was still breathing when I left him."

She sagged. *Thank God.*

She had no idea where they were, or where he was heading, but she needed to slow him down. She glanced around. He was carrying her from a car. Her heart squeezed. They were at a small airport. She saw a low, single terminal in the distance, and several parked planes.

Oh no. If he got on a plane...

She wriggled. She surprised him and she got free. Her feet hit the tarmac, and she punched him.

He barely reacted and lunged for her.

Addie stumbled back, heading for the small terminal. "Help! I need—"

Kozlov lifted her off her feet. She struggled and tried to bite him.

"Enough, Adaline," he growled. "You'll hurt the babies."

She stilled. *Dammit.*

His dark eyes bored into her. He touched a strand of her hair, stroking it. "So beautiful."

He sounded strange. His eyes had a weird look in them as he stared at her. She swallowed. He wasn't mentally healthy. He needed help.

"Kozlov—"

"Ilya. You will call me Ilya."

She swallowed. "Ilya, you can't take someone against their will. I'm in love with another man. I don't want to be with you."

His face hardened. "You will love me in time."

"I'm sure there is someone out there for you—"

"*No.* I know you are mine." A muscle ticked in his jaw. "We are destined for each other. I will protect and provide for you."

She bit her lip. There was no reasoning with him.

He leaned down and she tensed. He rubbed his nose against hers.

Oh, God.

"You will be my wife, Adaline. Now, I am taking you home."

He lifted her again and strode across the tarmac. She saw several small planes, and then a man stepped out from behind one, wiping his hands on a cloth. He was older, with a grizzled, weathered face. He barely spared her a glance before turning to Kozlov. They spoke to each other in Russian.

The newcomer nodded and jerked his head at the plane.

"We are almost ready, Adaline." Kozlov set her down.

"For what?" she whispered.

"The last leg of our journey." He smiled. "Your friends will not find us. I've made sure of it."

She had no idea where she was, or where they were going, but she prayed Bram and the Sentinel Security team did.

He'd find her. She knew he would.

She had to hold on to that.

Kozlov suddenly pressed a hand over her stomach, and she tried to jerk away. But he grabbed her.

"I can't wait to see you round with *my* child." An eager look filled his eyes.

Addie tasted bile in her throat. "Where are we going?"

"Far away. Close to my friends."

Her heart thumped.

"Get in the plane, Adaline, or I'll carry you aboard."

She steeled her spine, holding one hand protectively over hers and Bram's babies.

I'll protect you.

We just need to wait for daddy to find us.

THE ROOM HAD BEEN CONVERTED into a makeshift command center.

Hex had rented them rooms at a small motel near Hickory Ridge, then set up several laptops. She was hunched over one, absorbed in her searches. Her hands never stopped moving, data filling the screens.

There was no sign of Kozlov or Addie.

The bastard had disappeared like a ghost with Addie.

Addie. Bram squeezed his hands into fists. Pain was an aching throb inside him, tangled with rage and guilt.

He drew in a sharp breath. He didn't have the luxury of brooding. He had to find Addie.

Killian was on the phone, barking questions at someone. Devyn was on her own laptop, her brow creased. Matteo and Nick were out questioning people in case anyone had seen Kozlov.

Shade leaned against the wall, peering over Hex's shoulder.

"Got anything yet?" Shade asked.

"Step back." Hex elbowed the spy in the gut.

Shade just grinned at her.

"Go and be useful," Hex snapped. "Or do your skills only involve standing around looking hot while everyone else does the work?"

Shade's smile widened. "You think I'm hot?"

Hex rolled her bi-colored eyes and looked back at her screen.

"Hex, update?" Killian asked.

She tossed Shade a withering look before looking at her boss. "After being released after Mikhailov went down, Kozlov disappeared. Totally off grid. He was gone for a couple of months before he popped up in New York, and rented the apartment and storage space."

Killian frowned. "Where was he?"

"I don't know yet." A determined glint filled Hex's gaze. "But I *will* find him."

"He would've gone somewhere he felt comfortable." Shade crossed his arms. "If he was setting up a home, he'd want friends or allies close by."

Hex cocked her head and nodded. "Other Russians?"

"Could be," Shade agreed.

Her hands flew across the keyboard. "We know he didn't leave the country. I'm doing a search of the largest Russian communities in the USA. Then I'll cross-reference and see if he traveled to any of these places. He had to have called someone, visited someone."

Bram's hands flexed. He felt like everything was taking too long.

Was Addie okay? Afraid? Hurt? Tired?

God, what if Kozlov hurt the babies?

Pain threatened to close Bram's throat.

"Easy." Devyn gripped his arm. "Don't you dare lose hope, Bram. She needs you. She needs her tough, gruff man to bring her home."

Bram managed a nod.

She smiled and squeezed his arm. "We've got this." Her face sharpened. "And Kozlov is going to regret all of his life choices." She gave Bram's arm another squeeze and moved back to her laptop.

Killian was on the phone again. Bram glanced around the room. Shade was gone. He must have slipped out. "Where's Shade?"

Hex lifted her head, brow creased. "What do I look like? His babysitter?"

Bram eyed her. "Do you need some caffeine?"

She blew out a breath, ruffling her dark hair. "Maybe."

He snagged a soda from the stash of supplies they'd grabbed earlier. He cracked it and handed it over.

"What can I do to help?" he asked her.

Hex pointed at another laptop, taking a sip of the drink. "Go through those emails."

Bram waded through an email account that Hex said belonged to Kozlov. It was full of fishing and hunting information. Specs on different gun and hunting knives.

He tried not to think of Addie, hurt and afraid.

"I think I found something." Hex turned in her seat. "Kozlov emailed a friend in Alaska a few months back."

"Alaska?" Bram said.

She nodded. "It has one of the largest Russian communities in all of the country."

"It's isolated," Killian said. "He could easily keep to himself."

And hide a kidnapped woman. Bram pointed at his computer screen. "Plus, it's clear he likes hunting."

The door to the room opened, and Shade appeared. "I found the car Kozlov was driving."

Bram surged up. "Where?"

"An airport two hours away. Calhoun. Car was abandoned there. A contact just called me. No one matching Kozlov's description, with or without a woman, was listed on any of the commercial flights that left that airport today."

"I'll check charter operators." Hex's fingers danced over her keyboard. "Wait. There's one there called Krasny Air."

"Russian," Bram said.

"Yes. A flight left for Montana." She bounced in her chair. "God, there's another flight itinerary. After Montana, they're heading to Anchorage, Alaska."

Bram felt energy surge through him. "He's taking her to Alaska."

"I'll get the jet ready," Killian said. "Ric's feeling better, and is good to fly. Hex, see if you can find any real estate linked to Kozlov in Alaska." Killian frowned. "Do we have any contacts in Anchorage?"

She shook her head, then frowned, thoughtfully. "Wait. We do know someone who's spent some time up there working and fishing."

"Who?" Bram asked.

"Boone Hendrix."

The name sounded familiar, but Bram couldn't place him.

"Former Ghost Ops," Killian said. "He used to be on Vander Norcross' team."

Hex nodded. "He lives in Vermont now."

"Call him." Killian looked at Bram. "Let's bring Addie home."

CHAPTER SIXTEEN

Addie jerked against Kozlov as he dragged her off the plane.

"Stop it," he snapped.

She bared her teeth at him. She was tired, scared, gritty-eyed, and hungry. The plane journey to Alaska felt like it had taken forever. The plane had been smaller and far less luxurious than the Sentinel Security jet. They'd stopped to refuel somewhere, and he'd given her some food, but she'd only picked at it.

Cool air hit her, and she shivered. It was summer, but still much cooler here than in New York. Her leggings and shirt weren't quite enough protection. She turned her head and saw the line of majestic mountains in the distance. If only she was here for different reasons and could enjoy the view.

Kozlov tugged her along. She saw a big, silver truck with rugged tires waiting for them, a man standing beside it. He was of medium height, with a shaved head. He eyed her and she shivered. He had dead eyes.

He and Kozlov spoke in rapid-fire Russian.

"Everything is ready for us, Adaline," Kozlov said with a smile.

"You won't get away with this," she said. "Bram will come for me."

Kozlov glared at her. "Not if he can't find you. I've planned this for months. Covered my tracks. O'Donovan will never find you."

A ball lodged in her throat.

Her captor's smile was cold. "And soon, I'll arrange a little accident for the man who touched what is mine."

Her heart hit her ribs. "You're a monster."

"I'm not. I'm just a man who does what he must. I've always been good at getting the job done." He opened the back of the truck and shoved her inside.

Addie sat in the backseat and watched Anchorage slide by through the windows. The two men talked in Russian, laughing occasionally.

She rubbed her belly. "It'll be okay, babies," she whispered. She had to believe that. Kozlov wasn't smarter than the Sentinel Security team.

Bram would find her.

Soon, they were driving out of the town. The natural beauty was breathtaking. The mountains in the distance only had a tiny bit of snow on top of them, but were still striking, and all the trees were green. Pretty, purple wildflowers dotted the grass.

They drove for a while, the dirt road rough in places. Addie gripped the door to try and stop herself bouncing around. Kozlov finally turned off, following a rough track through thick trees. She watched an animal—a deer—dart across the road and into the bushes.

Then, the cabin came into view. It wasn't huge. It was made of brown logs with a green roof, and a large, wraparound porch. It was nestled into the trees beside a lake.

In any other circumstances, she'd think it was a nice place to visit.

The truck stopped. Another man, this one with a rifle resting on his shoulder, appeared from around the corner of the cabin. He wore jeans, a drab-green shirt, and a ratty ball cap.

Kozlov got out and opened the door for her. "Come. See your new home."

Addie gingerly slid out of the truck.

"See the beautiful view." He waved an arm proudly.

She took in the stunning mountains that sat on the other side of a small lake.

"I'll show you the cabin." He took her arm, calling out to the other two men.

She tried to pull free, but his grip tightened painfully.

"You will show me respect, Adaline, especially in front of my men." His tone was clipped. "I've done so much for you."

"You're crazy. You've *kidnapped* me. I don't want to be with you."

His face hardened, and he dragged her toward the building.

"Don't try to run. My men will be around. Plus, I have lots of security features on my land. If you run into any...boom."

Addie's stomach dropped.

"There are bears and other wildlife around, as well." He towed her up the steps and opened the front door.

The inside was cozy, but plain. There were simple brown couches in the living area, a round, wooden table with four chairs, and a snug kitchen. The window over the sink had a view of the lake.

"There are two bedrooms, but you will sleep with me," Kozlov announced.

Addie felt sick at the thought. "No."

He shook her. "You will do as I say."

"I'm not a doll, or possession. I make my own choices."

He moved fast, backing her up, and her pulse jumped. Her shoulder blades hit the wall, and he penned her in with his much bigger body.

"You're *mine*. That's all you are. You get no choices. You will obey me or..." His hand brushed over her stomach.

Rage pooled inside her and she glared at him. She wouldn't let him hurt her babies.

He leaned closer and she felt his hot breath on her cheek. She turned her head, and his lips touched her jaw.

"You can go to the bedroom and think." He stepped back. "Don't go outside. If you run, I will hunt you down." He cocked his head. "You will forget him, *milaya*. I promise."

He shoved her in the bedroom, and slammed the door.

A sob welled. Addie's chest was so tight. She made herself look at the room. There was a wooden-framed bed, with plaid covers. The window had another pretty view that she was too sick to take in.

She wrapped her arms around herself.

"It's okay, babies. It's going to be okay."

She was trapped with a madman, but she couldn't, she *wouldn't*, give up.

She had too much to live for.

She closed her eyes and thought of Bram.

THEIR JET WAS PARKED on a small, private airstrip in Vermont. Everything around them was vibrant green, bursting with life for the summer. Bram fought back his edginess as he waited, squirming slightly in his seat.

He wanted to get to Alaska. *Now.*

He looked out the window. Killian stalked down the steps toward a man waiting beside a battered truck.

Boone Hendrix was tall, with brown hair, and an All-American look. Bram would guess he'd been the quarterback of his school football team. He had broad shoulders, long legs, and wore a red flannel shirt, jeans, and boots.

He lifted his chin and shook Killian's hand.

"He's a good guy," Nick said, from the seat across the aisle. "Was a hell of a soldier."

Bram knew Hendrix would have been special forces, and to get selected for Ghost Ops, you had to be the best of the best.

"He has a farm up here," Nick continued, "but he does odd jobs, mostly for friends. Keeps his skills sharp. Norcross uses him occasionally."

Bram knew these odd jobs didn't require hammers or saws.

Shade shifted in his seat. "I've heard of him. Good reputation. He keeps in touch with a few of his former Ghost Ops buddies."

"He was in New York last year to help out Remi and Maverick Rivera," Nick added.

Bram nodded. He watched as Boone pulled a duffel bag out of the back of his truck, then opened the passenger-side door.

A large German Shepherd leaped out.

The handsome dog wasn't just a pet. In an instant, Bram could see the animal was well-trained and fit.

Soon the men and dog boarded the plane.

"Everyone," Killian said. "This is Boone Hendrix, and Atlas. Boone, let me introduce you to everyone, starting with my wife."

"Wife?" Boone said, eyebrows rising. "When did this happen?"

"Recently." Devyn stepped forward, holding out a hand. "I'm Devyn."

As Boone shook her hand, Atlas sat in the aisle, eyeing her.

Devyn looked down at him. "Hello, handsome."

The dog nudged her, and she gave him a pat.

"Careful," Boone warned. "He looks tough, but he loves to beg for treats."

The man shook everyone's hand. Bram was last.

"Sorry to hear about your woman," Boone said.

"Her name's Addie." Bram nodded. "Thanks for helping."

"I'll do everything I can to help you find her."

"Let's get airborne," Killian said.

By the time they'd reached cruising altitude, the team was deep in discussion with Boone.

"I've messaged a few of my buddies in Anchorage," Boone said. "Asked if anyone's seen this Kozlov. I know some of the local Russians. Most are decent and hard-working, but there are plenty who aren't. Most of them are into poaching and illegal hunting."

"We're pretty sure Kozlov has a house or a cabin there," Hex said, letting out a frustrated sigh. "I can't find anything in his name."

"Kozlov is good at hiding his tracks when he needs to," Devyn said.

"He's there," Bram said. "Somewhere."

Another hour passed, and Boone checked his phone. "I've got something. A buddy of mine works at the Ted Stevens, Anchorage's airport." He lifted his gaze. "He saw your guy."

Bram's spine locked. "He's there?"

"Yep. Flew in today with...a blonde woman."

Bram barely suppressed a growl.

"Keep a lock on it, Bram," Killian warned.

"Someone met them at the plane." Boone smiled. "Hex, I have the license plate number of the truck they left in for you."

"Ooh, gimme." Hex tapped on her keyboard. "I've got it! The truck is registered to a company called Dom Services."

"Dom means home in Russian," Killian said.

Hex tapped some more, then pumped a fist into the

air. "I have an address of a cabin just outside of Anchorage on some land."

"Find some aerial photos," Killian said. "And pull up any information you can on the building."

Hex worked fast. Boone and Bram leaned over the table, looking at the computer screen. The images showed a small wood cabin by a lake.

This was it. Bram could feel it.

"Let's plan some reconnaissance," Killian said.

SEVERAL HOURS LATER, clad in cargo pants and a tactical vest, Bram threw a duffel bag in the back of a mud-splattered GMC Yukon.

They'd landed in Anchorage, and two vehicles had been waiting for them. Both were streaked with mud and looked like they fit in. They didn't want to announce their presence to Kozlov.

He shifted impatiently, waiting for the others to follow. He scanned the airport, wondering which plane had brought Addie here.

I'm close, Addie. Just hold on a little bit longer.

Soon, Bram found himself in the back of one Yukon, with Atlas panting beside him. Boone sat on the other side of his dog.

Killian and Devyn were in front, with Killian driving. Nick, Matteo, Shade and Hex were in the other vehicle.

"We'll head to a location east of the property, and go in on foot." Devyn was looking at a map on a tablet.

"There's a good vantage point here." She pointed. "It's on higher ground."

Killian met Bram's gaze in the rearview mirror. "We can't go in until the time is right. Until we have the right intel we need. Kozlov is no rookie."

"I get it," Bram bit out.

"Even if you see her, Bram, you have to keep your cool. Her life could depend on it."

"I know."

Killian nodded. "Let's do this."

The other SUV was right behind them, and they all stopped at the location Devyn had picked.

Everyone got out, all dressed the same as Bram. Hex opened the trunk of her SUV, and opened her box containing her drone. She opened a laptop.

"I have the drone ready to go, but I can't risk a flyover of the cabin. I don't want to alert Kozlov by getting the drone too close."

Killian frowned. "Get it in the air, but stay back for now."

Hex nodded. "Go bring our girl home."

A second later, there was a whirr of sound as the drone flared to life and lifted into the air. Hex was focused on the laptop, controlling the device as it disappeared into the sky.

Matteo, Nick, and Shade went in one direction, disappearing into the trees. Devyn, Killian, Bram, and Boone, along with Atlas, moved off in another. They moved quickly through the trees.

The trees were dense, and everything was green and crisp.

Bram gripped his rifle and breathed deeply. Addie was close. He had to stay in control.

They trudged up a hill and startled a large hare. It hopped off into the bushes.

"Here," Devyn said.

They all crouched at the crest of the hill. The lake glinted down below, and Bram spotted a floatplane and a small boat resting beside a small dock.

The cabin was made of logs, with a simple design and deck on one side. Atlas made a low sound.

A guard appeared, circling the cabin, a rifle on his shoulder. He was smoking a cigarette.

It didn't look like he was expecting trouble.

"There's a second guard closer to the lake," Devyn murmured.

Bram moved his head and saw the other man. He had a ball cap on his head.

Two guards and Kozlov.

"Hex, heat signatures?" Killian asked through his earpiece.

"I can't get too close," Hex responded. "But it looks like two outside and two inside."

"We need to confirm she's here," Killian said.

Bram stared at the cabin and lifted a pair of binoculars. There were curtains on some windows. He couldn't see anyone.

Come on, Kozlov.

"There's a door opening to the side deck," Hex said suddenly.

Bram swiveled the binoculars and saw Ilya Kozlov appear. His pulse jumped.

There you are, asshole.

The man was talking to someone inside, then he yanked a woman out of the cabin.

Addie.

Bram jerked, and both Devyn and Boone grabbed him.

"I'm not moving," he gritted out.

He watched Addie stomp to the railing of the deck. She was still in the leggings and shirt she'd worn to Georgia. Her hair was loose, the breeze setting it dancing. He could see she was tense, but also mad.

Despite his frustration, his lips twitched. *That's my girl.*

She wasn't hurt. That was the main thing.

Kozlov came up behind her and touched her hair. She tried to jerk away. The man snapped at her.

Addie went still, her body stiff, and her lips pressed into a flat line.

Kozlov stroked a hand down her arm, and Bram's fingers tightened on his rifle. Then Kozlov leaned closer, nuzzling his face against her hair.

I will kill you, Kozlov. I promise.

Addie kept her gaze on the surroundings, turning her head until it looked like she was looking right at Bram.

Hold on, sunshine.

CHAPTER SEVENTEEN

"Dinner will be ready soon." Kozlov looked over at her from the stove and smiled.

Addie didn't respond. She sat at the table, her hands twisted together. Whatever he was cooking didn't smell bad, but her stomach was in too many knots to let her eat.

He'd put some wildflowers on the table. Like they were on a date. Like he was trying to woo her, or something.

He was sick. He needed help.

She needed to try and get a message to Bram and the others.

Her gaze fell to Kozlov's cellphone, resting on the table. Her muscles twitched. If she could only find a way to use his phone. She licked her lips. She could tell Bram where she was, and warn them that Kozlov had the place booby-trapped.

"You'll like this. It's called *shchi*. Good Russian food. The recipe was my mother's." He stirred the pan.

When he glanced at Addie, she managed a nod.

"There is good hunting here. I have lots of meat in the freezer. Deer, elk, rabbit." There was a knock at the front door, and he scowled. "My men."

"Go. I'll be right here." *Because you kidnapped me.*

Kozlov wiped his hands and headed for the door. When his back was turned, she snatched the phone. She quickly followed Hex's instructions for hacking a phone, her hands shaking.

Come on. Focus. She pulled in a breath. *There.* She'd gotten it open.

Quickly, she tapped in the Sentinel Security emergency number.

Cabin. Lake. Near Anchorage. Two guards. Place booby-trapped with bombs.

She hit send and glanced at the door. Kozlov was still talking to his men.

Come on. Finally, the phone showed the message had sent.

Relief hit her. She deleted any record of the message and set the phone back in place. Damn, the screen was still lit up.

Go back to sleep. She willed the screen to go dark. Her heart punched against her ribs like she'd gone ten rounds with a heavyweight boxer.

Kozlov turned.

God, she needed to distract him. She stood. "Dinner smells good."

He smiled at her. "*Da.* You're hungry?"

"And thirsty." She circled the table and blocked his view of the phone. "Can I have some water?"

He eyed her for a second. Could he hear her heart pounding?

He opened a cabinet and took out a glass. He poured her a drink of water and came straight to her. "Here, *milaya.*"

"Thanks." *Please, let the phone have gone dark.* She sipped the water, trying to look calm.

Kozlov eyed her for a second. "Sit."

With a shaky breath, she shifted. When she glanced down at the table, the phone screen was dark.

She released a slightly shaky breath.

"Adaline." He grabbed her arm and her heartrate spiked. "You are so beautiful." He cupped the side of her face and she tensed. "You will love me."

"That's not how love works, Ilya," she said.

Kozlov's smile evaporated, a groove forming in his brow. His fingers tightened on her skin until they hurt. She gasped.

"I *will* make you love me." He lowered his head.

She tried to jerk back, but he held her tighter. She didn't want to kiss him. "Stop!"

"Never." His mouth hit the corner of hers. She felt his tongue on her skin. "I will show you how good we can be."

A sob escaped her, and she shoved at him.

They scuffled, bumping into the kitchen counter. His mouth moved across her cheek, his fingers digging into her hip.

"Tonight, I will have you naked." He bit the side of her neck.

God, no. Her pulse galloped. She didn't want him touching her. She only wanted Bram.

"I like it rough, *milaya*. You can handle me. Maybe it will solve the problem of another man's babies inside you."

Bile filled her mouth. He wasn't ever going to hurt her babies. She wouldn't let him.

Her hands moved against the counter, looking for something she could use to fend him off. Her fingers closed on the handle of an empty frypan that he hadn't used. It was heavy, made of cast iron.

He pulled her closer and she grimaced. She felt his hard erection grind against her stomach.

No.

She hefted the frypan and swung it at his head.

It connected with a sickening crunch. His head lifted, and their gazes met for a horrifying second, then he collapsed.

He hit the floor with a thump.

Shit, shit, shit.

She set the pan down and stepped over him. She raced to the bedroom and found her shoes. She pulled them on, hopping a little, then she sprinted to the front door.

The need to escape thumped hard inside her.

Wait. Think, Addie. She forced herself to take a few breaths.

She pushed the curtain at the window aside and peered outside. She needed to avoid the guards.

She was horribly aware that there were booby-traps

out there. She'd need to be very careful, but she sure as hell wasn't staying here.

It was still light outside, even though it was getting late. She was thankful it wasn't winter. She didn't want to be running around in the dark. Still, could she make it back to Anchorage? Despair hit her. She knew it was dangerous to wander out in this wild wilderness.

She rubbed her belly. "We're getting out of here, babies. We've got this."

She spotted a guard. He was strolling slowly, walking past the cabin. He didn't stop or slow down.

Carefully, she cracked open the front door. There was no sign of the other guard anywhere. She hoped he'd turned in for the night.

Addie crept out, praying the steps wouldn't creak under her weight. She kept her gaze on the guard's back. She reached the bottom and angled away from him, trying to move quietly.

How long would Kozlov stay unconscious?

Her hindbrain screamed at her. *Run. Run. Run.*

She looked at the rough track leading up to the cabin. She knew there were no booby-traps on the road, but it was also too open. They'd see her and chase her down easily.

She had to risk going through the trees. Her stomach churned.

The guard stopped. She had to go. *Now.*

Addie turned and ran into the trees.

They swallowed her up, and she had no idea where she was going. She just knew that she had to get away from Kozlov.

She ran into a little clearing. A circle of churned-up earth sat in the center of it, and she skirted around it. Metal glinted from inside the dirt.

Crap. It had to be one of Kozlov's "security measures." She gave it a wide berth and kept going.

Branches slapped at her, and twigs snapped under her shoes.

"Adaline!"

The angry bellow echoed through the trees.

Kozlov was conscious.

Fear filled her, her pulse fluttering. She ran faster, holding her stomach. She knew when he caught her, he wouldn't be gentle. He'd punish her for escaping.

She couldn't give up.

She raced through the trees. She just had to keep running.

Suddenly, something caught her foot, and she tripped over. She hit the ground hard, turning to her side at the last minute.

Oomph. Dazed, she looked down. There was a wire loosely tangled around her ankle.

Oh, crap. She kicked free, then pushed up, and kept running.

She hadn't gone far when—

Boom.

The blast lifted her off the ground, and slammed her down. She cradled her belly. *Oh, God.*

She looked back over her shoulder, and behind her, the trees were alight. Her breath caught in her lungs.

Breathe, Addie. Air rushed into her lungs. She wasn't hurt. Nothing was sprained. She had to keep moving.

Shakily, she pushed to her feet.

Shouts echoed through the trees, followed by a gunshot.

Kozlov and his goons were coming.

But Addie wasn't giving up.

BRAM WATCHED the guard strolling around the cabin area. He clenched his hand into a fist. He wanted to take the asshole down.

He stared at the cabin, and wished he knew what was happening inside.

"Bram!" Hex's frantic voice through his earpiece. "I just got a message from Addie."

"What?"

"A message from an unknown number to our emergency number. She must've found a phone."

Bram found himself warring between pride and worry. Kozlov wasn't stupid. She was taking a big risk using his phone. If he caught her...

"She said the grounds are booby-trapped," Hex said.

He heard Killian curse. It wasn't really a surprise.

"All right, I—" The cabin door opening caught Bram's attention.

His chest locked. *No.*

"Addie is on the move," Killian murmured.

Bram saw her glance at the guard, then take off running for the trees.

Fuck. Bram whipped his rifle up. If she hit a booby-trap...

"We need to intercept her," he barked.

"I'm moving the drone closer," Hex said. "It won't matter now if Kozlov knows we're here."

All of a sudden, Kozlov burst out of the cabin and roared Addie's name. Blood covered one side of his face.

His guard came running, pointing toward the trees. Bram lifted his rifle and took a shot.

The guard went down, and Kozlov moved fast. He sprinted for the trees, running after Addie.

"Move." Bram launched himself up and ran.

He heard the others right behind him. He slapped branches out of his way. He had to get to Addie.

Kozlov was a decent hunter. He'd easily be able to follow her trail.

"She's heading north," Hex said.

"We're circling around from the other side." Nick's voice came over their earpieces.

Atlas took off running ahead of them, moving fast. Boone sprinted right behind his dog.

An explosion cut through the air.

Bram stumbled. *Addie*. He could barely breathe.

"Hex?" His voice cracked.

"I see her! She's all right." Then the hacker cursed. "Kozlov is closing in on her."

Bram picked up speed.

"Stop!" Killian yelled.

Bram skidded to a stop. It was then he saw light glinting off a wire at neck height, strung between the trees. *Fuck*. It would have decapitated him.

He ducked under it.

"Bram, slow down," Killian said. "You'll be no good to her dead."

"If Kozlov catches her…"

"We aren't going to let that happen."

Bram kept moving, now at a slightly slower pace. But it nearly killed him.

Gunshots rang out. He dropped and heard bullets *thunk* into the tree trunks beside him. Devyn ducked behind a tree, her gun aimed at the other side of the clearing. Killian whirled behind a tree.

Where the hell was the shooter? Bram raised his head. It had to be the other guard.

More bullets. They hit the dirt near Bram's head, and he rolled.

There was a deep bark. Atlas sprinted across the clearing and leaped.

A second later, Bram heard a man curse, then start yelling.

Boone raced after his dog. Bram rose, and caught sight of a guard rolling in the dirt, trying to avoid Atlas. The dog was latched onto his arm, growling.

Boone kicked the guard, then leaned down and punched him in the face. The former soldier's features were set in blank lines. A warrior doing his job.

"I've got this," Boone said. "Go."

Bram glanced over at Devyn and Killian, then the three of them took off.

Bram weaved through the trees. "Hex, where is she?"

"She veered northeast. Kozlov is still after her. The guy is good, he's getting close."

"Wolf and the others?"

"We're coming," Nick replied.

"They're a little farther away than you," Hex said. "I'm moving in closer to see if I can detect any more booby traps."

Bram wanted to run faster, but he gritted his teeth and made himself check for traps. Killian and Devyn kept pace with him.

His team had his back.

He'd been alone when his ma and Fiona had been taken. Eighteen, untrained. He realized now that there was nothing he could've done. Their fate had been sealed by the three murderers who'd taken their lives.

But now, Bram had a team, he had skills. He'd save the woman he loved, and their growing babies.

He'd love her with everything he had, and learn what he needed to about being a husband and father.

Addie would help him.

His friends would help him.

"Guys, there's something buried in the clearing just ahead of you," Hex said. "Veer west."

Bram adjusted course.

Hold on just a little longer, sunshine, then you can hold on to me.

CHAPTER EIGHTEEN

A ddie ran through the trees, her chest heaving.

Kozlov was coming. She could hear him. He was hunting her.

She paused behind a tree, trying to hear over the thud of her heart. Her ears were still ringing from the explosion. She sucked in air.

"You've got this, Addie," she whispered.

Then she heard something. Her head jerked up. Something or someone was moving close by.

She bit her lip, spun, and ran in the other direction.

The noise followed her. Something crashed through the undergrowth. She whirled, then froze.

A black bear ambled out of the trees.

Oh. God.

Her blood ran cold. The bear paused and she felt like it was glaring at her.

Slowly, she backed up a step. It took a step closer.

Addie fought the urge to run. Then she heard the

sound of gunfire, not far away. Startled, the bear spun and ran off into the trees.

She turned and kept going in the opposite direction to the bear.

The ground sloped downward, and she skidded. Then she felt a flare of pain in her ankle, and fell.

Sitting on her butt in the dirt, she fought back her rising panic. What else could go wrong? She moved her leg.

"Ow, ow, ow." She rubbed her ankle. It hurt, but she knew it wasn't broken or badly sprained. Dancing had taught her how to gauge her injuries. She'd danced on sore ankles too many times to count.

She had to get up, she couldn't stop.

"I'm coming, Adaline." Kozlov's voice rang through the trees.

She gritted her teeth, gripped a nearby tree trunk, and hauled herself up. The asshole was taunting her.

Well, she wasn't letting him get to her.

She kept running. Her ankle throbbed, but she tried to block it out. Then she heard a strange whirring sound. She looked around, then up. A speck of black was floating above her, silhouetted against the darkening sky.

She gasped. It was a drone. Like the ones Hex used.

God, was Bram here with the team?

Hope burst through her, giving her a surge of energy. She hobbled down the hill, barely feeling her ankle now. She just had to hold on a little bit longer.

The ground flattened out, and she picked up speed. She heard a sound behind her.

"You can't escape me, Adaline."

God, Kozlov was getting closer.

She reached a small clearing and sprinted through it.

Twang.

Something hit her and wrapped around her body. She was yanked off her feet.

She cried out. Panting, she found herself hanging a few feet off the ground, wrapped in a rope net.

She'd been caught in a trap.

No. *No.*

Addie wriggled and tried to get free, but managed to do nothing more than just swing slightly back and forth.

Dammit.

She squeezed her eyes shut, choking back her panic. Bram was coming. She was sure of it.

A twig cracked nearby, and she opened her eyes.

Kozlov stepped out of the trees, a big, black gun in his hand.

Her mouth went dry.

His gaze locked on her. "Adaline, I am very disappointed."

She stayed silent.

He strode closer, his eyes alight, and his face twisted. "The man who dared touch you is here."

Everything inside her leaped. Bram was here. He was coming.

Kozlov's scowl deepened, but Addie couldn't stop her smile.

"You have not appreciated what I've done for you, for us," he said.

"I never wanted this, or you."

He nodded slowly.

"Please, just let me go," she said.

"No. But I will leave. They won't ever catch me, but... you are mine, Adaline."

Dammit. He wasn't going to give up. Her stomach sank.

He leaned closer to her. "And if I can't have you, no one will."

She blinked. *What?*

She watched him slide the gun away. Her hands twined around the rope. "Ilya—"

He shook his head. "It's too late, Adaline." He pulled out a hunting knife.

Her lungs locked. It was huge, with a serrated blade.

"We will be together in the next life," he said.

"Please, don't do this. I'm pregnant—" She struggled, sending the net swinging wildly. "Please."

He lifted the knife.

A large shape sprinted out of the trees, flew through the air, and tackled Kozlov to the ground.

The two men went down, wrestling in the dirt.

Addie sucked air into her lungs, fighting back a wild rush of panic.

It was Shade. His tawny hair had come loose, spilling around his shoulders as he punched Kozlov.

The fight was brutal, and deep grunts filled the clearing.

Kozlov got up on one knee and sliced out with his knife.

Shade hissed, pressing a hand to his bicep. Blood oozed between his fingers. Then he whirled and jumped. His hard kick sent a boot slamming into Kozlov's face.

Kozlov cursed and pulled back. He yanked something off his belt and held it up.

Oh, no. "Shade, he's got a grenade!"

Shade dove, and tackled Kozlov again. His hand snapped out, and she heard Kozlov's wrist break.

Her captor roared and dropped the grenade.

Shade lunged and caught it. He spun and threw it like a star baseball pitcher.

It sailed into the trees.

And detonated.

The shockwave rippled through the air, and she closed her eyes. *God.*

Kozlov straightened, his gun in his hand. He smiled, blood on his teeth.

Shade started to move, but she knew he couldn't outrun a gun.

Bang. Bang.

Addie jerked. *No.*

But it was Kozlov who jolted. Bram walked out of the trees, a rifle in his hands, with the butt pressed to his shoulder. He had it aimed straight at Kozlov.

He fired again, and Kozlov dropped his gun, then fell to his knees.

"Mine," Kozlov gritted out.

"She was never yours." Bram fired again and Kozlov toppled.

Addie let out a sob.

It was over.

The Sentinel Security team poured out of the trees, including a handsome, rugged man she didn't recognize, with a huge German Shepherd by his side.

Then Bram strode to her. His hands curled around hers on the ropes.

"Addie? Are you hurt?"

She shook her head. She could see that fear and worry had etched deep grooves into his face.

He slid a hand through the net to cup her cheek. "You're all right?"

She pressed her cheek into his palm. "I am now." She smiled at the man she loved. "I knew you'd come."

***

"HOLD ON, ADDIE." Bram pulled out his knife. He had to cut her free.

"Bram?"

He met her gaze.

"I'm not afraid anymore," she said.

His gut clenched. He started sawing through the rope.

"Is she okay?" Killian asked.

"I'm fine." There were tears in her eyes even though she was smiling. "You all came."

"We sure did," Devyn said.

They helped him cut her free of the net and he pulled her out. She stood, then winced.

"What?" He cupped her shoulders.

"I think I sprained my ankle. It's not—"

He scooped her off her feet. Finally, Addie was in his arms.

Bram felt a ball of pressure in his chest. She was safe.

Alive. Breathing. He dropped to the ground, cradling her on his lap.

"I've got you." He rocked her.

"I know." She wound her arms around him and hugged him back.

That pressure in his chest eased a little. "I'm sorry he got you."

"It *wasn't* your fault." She framed his face. "Bad things happen, Bram. You can't control every little thing. The important thing is that it's over."

He nodded, then pressed a hand over her belly and felt one of the babies kick. He pressed his mouth to hers, savoring the feel of her lips under his.

She made a small sound, and leaned into him, kissing him back.

"Nothing like a happy ending," Boone murmured.

"I'm not happy," Shade said. "I'm bleeding."

"Come here, you big baby," Devyn said. "Let me look at your scratch."

"It's a gash, Hellfire," Shade insisted.

"Is everyone all right?" Hex's voice came through their earpieces. The drone hovered overhead.

"We're all fine, Hex," Killian replied.

Bram pressed his forehead to Addie's. She had dirt smeared on one cheek, but was still the most beautiful woman in the world.

"I love you, Addie."

She sucked in a breath. "*Bram.*"

"I should've told you sooner, but I'm not very good with words. But I think being with you, you'll help me."

He caressed her stomach. "I want our babies to know how much I love them. I never want them to doubt it."

"You'll be a great dad, Bram."

"Because I have you at my side."

She smiled. "I love you, too."

"Sunshine." He kissed her again.

"Ow, Devyn, you're worse than the cut," Shade complained.

Bram lifted his head and saw Devyn pressing a bandage over the man's injury. Blood had soaked into the sleeve of his shirt.

"It's just temporary," Devyn said. "It needs to be disinfected and glued, but this will hold you for a bit."

"Guys," Hex said. "I've rented us hotel rooms in Anchorage. We can rest and get cleaned up before the flight home."

Atlas barked.

"Yeah, sounds good to me too, buddy." Boone rubbed the top of his dog's head.

Bram carried Addie carefully back to the SUV.

"If it's okay with you, I don't want to plan any Alaskan vacations," she murmured.

He kissed the top of her head. "I'll take you wherever you want to go."

She smiled. "Maybe a short babymoon before the twins arrive, because after that, we're probably not going to have a lot of time for vacations." She met his gaze. "I wouldn't mind a trip to Ireland."

He could see her there, soaking up the history, tapping a foot to live music at the pub. He thought of all the places he'd like to take her.

"And you should tell your father he's going to be a grandfather," she said.

Bram grunted. He'd think about it.

"Bram?"

He blew out a breath. "Fine."

She smiled at him.

He got her settled in the back of the SUV. Atlas jumped in, tail wagging.

"Hello." Addie smiled at the dog. "Who's this?"

"This is Atlas. He and his owner, Boone, are friends. They came to help find you."

She patted Atlas' head. "Thanks, Atlas."

Boone slid into the front seat and smiled back. "It's our pleasure. Glad you're okay."

Addie leaned against Bram. "I'm better than okay. All my dreams have come true. I can't ask for more than that."

Bram breathed her in. He'd never been anyone's dream before, and he liked it.

CHAPTER NINETEEN

Addie felt awesome.

She was wearing cozy, warm clothes that Hex had brought for her. She'd had a hot shower and food at the hotel in Anchorage. Bram had strapped her ankle and rubbed antiseptic cream on her scratches.

And now he was holding her tight against him in the back of the SUV. They were currently driving to Anchorage Airport to fly back to New York. Through the window, she spotted the Sentinel Security jet.

"How's Ric?" she asked.

"He's fine," Killian said from the front seat. "Eager to see you. He blames himself for letting Kozlov take you."

She rolled her eyes. It seemed that the Sentinel Security heroes were always shouldering the blame for everything.

Bram kissed the top of her head. "Ready to go home?"

"So ready." She'd had more than enough adventure.

Once they stopped beside the jet, he helped her out

of the vehicle and held her hand up the stairs. The others started loading gear into the cargo area.

She heard raised voices inside the jet.

"Would you hold still?" Hex snapped.

"That hurts." Shade's voice.

"It's killing the germs that will infect your stupid body." Hex huffed. "Maybe I should let you die of an infection."

"I don't think you want that, pixie."

Bram tried to urge Addie inside, but she held up her hand to stop him.

Hex made an annoyed sound. "That is a dumb nickname. Now, stop being a baby. I thought you were a tough spy."

"I think you're enjoying this."

Hex snorted. "Hold still for the glue." A pause. "Take your shirt off. It'll be easier. And I see that smirk, James Bond. If you make a joke about me wanting you naked, I'll smack you."

There was a low, sexy chuckle. "There, shirt off." Now there was silence. "If you look at me like that, I'll make the joke." Shade's voice had lowered to a drawl. "A little smacking could be fun."

Bram pressed closer and heard the conversation inside. "Ah, hell."

"I'm busy looking at your cut." The hacker's tone was withering.

"Don't interrupt them." Addie leaned inside, peering around the corner into the jet.

The pair were sitting at the back of the aircraft. Shade had his shirt off, and...wow. Addie loved Bram—his wide chest, strong body, smattering of red hair. But Shade was every woman's fantasy. Bronze skin taut over smooth, hard muscles, and too many ridges on his abdomen to count.

Hex was standing beside him in dark jeans and a red, long-sleeved T-shirt. The woman was working on the cut high up on Shade's muscular bicep.

"That tickles," Shade said.

"Quit complaining, or I'll glue your lips together." Hex brandished the tube.

Addie bit her lip to keep from laughing.

Shade's voice lowered even more. "I think you'd prefer I use my lips to do other things."

Hex leaned closer, and Shade's gaze locked on her.

"Hold still," she said.

"Fuck you smell good, Jet."

Addie saw Hex freeze.

"Shut up, Shade." Hex's voice was an unconvincing whisper.

Suddenly, the man yanked her into his lap.

"If you tear that glue—"

Shade's mouth cut off her words.

Addie grinned and slapped a hand over her mouth.

"What are they doing now?" Bram muttered.

"Shh," she said.

Hex slid her hands into Shade's hair, pulling it out of its bun. Her moan mingled with his groan.

God, they looked good together. Tiny Hex against the big, bad spy.

"Addie." Bram stepped forward, crowding her. When he saw Hex and Shade, he scowled. "Fuck."

Unfortunately, Bram's voice was loud enough for the kissing pair to hear.

Hex wrenched her mouth off Shade's and leaped to her feet. She shot Addie and Bram a glance, smoothing her hands down her jeans. Then she glared at the spy. "Do that again, and I will hack your bank account and drain it."

Shade grinned at her, cocky as hell. "Which one?"

"All of them." She threw the tube of medical glue at him, then stalked up the aisle of the jet. "Glad you're okay, Addie."

"Thanks, Hex."

The tech guru swept off the jet.

Bram moved to a seat and sat without a word.

Addie looked at Shade. He winked at her.

Bram pulled her down onto the seat beside him.

"That was...spicy," she whispered.

Her man grunted and she smiled.

Soon, the others filed onto the jet. Shade, unfortunately, had put his shirt back on, and Addie noticed that Hex sat as far from him as was possible.

"Feeling okay?" Bram asked.

"Yes. I'm glad it's all over." She was determined to put Kozlov out of her mind and not spare any more energy on him.

Bram spread his palm over her belly. "We need to turn my spare room into a nursery."

She smiled. "Are you asking me to move in with you?"

His brow creased. "Yes."

"Then yes, I will. I hope you can still find space to do your carvings. Will you carve something for the babies?"

He nodded.

"Maybe you should think of showing them to someone?" she suggested.

"Showing them?" He looked confused.

"To a gallery? Maybe your friend Eamon Farley."

Her man's scowl deepened. "It's just a hobby."

One he was brilliant at. Hmm, she'd need to work on him. She slid a hand up his cheek. "I love you, Bram 'Excalibur' O'Donovan. You're going to be an amazing father."

"I'll do everything I can to be the best father possible. I'll protect them, and you." He pulled her closer. "I'll love them, and you. You burrowed inside me, sunshine. You make me a better man. I want you, not because you're pregnant or because of any sense of duty, but because you're here." He moved her hand to his chest. "I feel you here every day. Every battered bit of my soul is yours."

Tears made her eyes prickle as love welled inside her. "I love you exactly as you are, Bram. From the moment I first saw you, I felt it. My heart is yours."

One week later

BRAM SMOOTHED the tool over the wood, then sat back. It was finished.

The sculpture was of two toddlers—a boy and a girl. They were giggling at each other.

He stood. Since they'd returned from Alaska, he'd moved his carving gear in the small office nook off the living room. There was just enough space for him to do his work. His sculptures of Addie were now in the bedroom. He'd made one of her with her growing belly, a serene smile on her face.

He carried the new one of the twins into his guest room. The nursery.

It smelled of fresh paint. He'd banned Addie from helping, but Nick and Matteo had pitched in. Addie had picked the soft-yellow color. There was no furniture yet, but it was on their To-Do list. They'd make this into a lovely space for their babies.

There was a small pile of baby things that he'd brought over from Addie's. He looked at one small suit, and could hardly believe how small it was. He moved over to the shelves and set the sculpture down. He had ideas for plenty more, and he could imagine tiny fingers stroking them.

He touched the giggling faces on the sculpture. "I can't wait to meet you both."

Thankfully, he wasn't quite as terrified of being a father anymore. He headed back to the office, and opened the drawer of his desk.

Inside was the sculpture he'd finished the day before. He smiled. He hoped Addie liked it.

He lifted it out, along with one other important item.

His phone rang, vibrating in his pocket. He pulled it

out and saw a video call from Hex. He muttered a curse and answered it.

On the screen he saw Hex, with Devyn, Hadley, and Matteo crowding in.

"Did you ask her yet?" Hex asked.

"No," he growled. "I was letting her sleep in. She was tired last night."

"It's so sweet how you look after her," Hadley said.

Bram would never get used to being described as sweet.

"I like seeing how sweet Addie tamed the grumpy Irish beast," Matteo said with a shit-eating grin.

"Go away," Bram muttered.

"Okay," Hex said. "Call us when you've done it." She blew a kiss. Behind her, Devyn gave him a thumbs-up.

Shaking his head, Bram headed for the bedroom. Addie was all moved in. She'd given up her apartment, and formally resigned from the job at *On the Rocks*. Paddy had told her she had a place there whenever she wanted it, and he wanted to see the twins when they arrived. Bram had watched her carefully over the last week to see if there was any leftover trauma from her ordeal with Kozlov. But she seemed happy.

Addie was good at that. Not dwelling on the bad things, and moving on. For now, she was focusing on the impending arrival of the twins, although she liked to hang out with Hex in the command center and give the tech guru a hand.

She'd spoken with her parents as well. They were recovering from their encounter with Kozlov, and seemed genuinely happy for Addie.

He opened the bedroom door.

The light was still on in the bathroom. It didn't bother him to sleep with it on. He knew she slept better with it. She was on her side in the bed, propped up with several pillows, and wearing one of his T-shirts. Her blonde hair was spread everywhere.

He felt a pang in his chest. Damn, he was a lucky bastard.

He sat beside her and stroked her bare leg.

She stirred, and when she saw him, she shot him a beautiful smile. "Morning."

"Morning, sunshine."

"Did you get up early?" She yawned.

"I got up to carve. I finished one for the babies."

Addie sat up and pressed a hand to her belly. "Well, I know Fiona and Murphy will love it."

Love flooded him. They'd decided—it had been Addie's idea—to name the twins after his mother and sister. Murphy had been his ma's maiden name.

"I love you, Addie." It was getting easier and easier to say the words.

"And I love you right back."

She was like a ray of sunshine in his bed. He knew he didn't deserve her, but he was never giving her up.

"I have something for you," she said.

He scowled. "I have something for you."

She smiled and reached over to open a drawer of the nightstand. "Me first."

She pulled out a frame and handed it to him. It was a picture of him, at around fifteen years old, with his ma and Fiona. Ma was smiling, Fiona was pulling a face at

Bram. He was being a stoic teenager, but he had a faint tilt to his lips.

"Where did you get this?"

"Your dad. I emailed him."

They'd spoken with him at the beginning of the week. Of course, Addie had charmed the old man. They'd promised to visit him after the babies were born.

"He said he has other photos. He misses them, too."

Bram ran a thumb over Fiona's face. Then he set the frame on the nightstand. Addie was helping him remember the good times, not just how he'd lost them.

"So, what have you got for me?" She raised a brow.

Nerves hit him like a wave. "Ah." *Feck, get it together, O'Donovan.*

He pulled out the carving.

She took it in her slim hands. One side was Addie in a pretty dress, her hands clasped together as she stared at the man on the other side. It was Bram, kneeling at her feet.

Holding up a ring.

"Bram, it's gorgeous. You finally did one of you, just like I wanted." Then she realized what it signified. She looked up with a gasp.

Bram knelt beside the bed, holding up a ring.

"This was my mother's, and my grandmother's before that." The ring was old-fashioned, with diamonds in a flower setting. "Addie, you're mine and I'm yours—"

"Yes." Tears ran down her cheeks. "Yes, Bram." She flew at him, and he caught her. "I love you."

He cleared his throat. "Just to be sure, you're agreeing to marry me."

She slapped a kiss on his cheek. "Yes!"

He slid the ring onto her finger. It fit her, like it was right where it was supposed to be.

"I'm yours, Bram." She put his hand on her stomach and entwined her fingers with his. "We're yours."

"And I'm never letting you go." As he kissed her, his phone started to ring. He knew it was Hex and their friends.

He pulled out the phone and thumbed it off, then he rolled Addie back onto the bed, listening to the sound of her vibrant laughter. A sound he wanted to listen to for the rest of his life.

EPILOGUE

Four and a half months later

B ram sipped his beer and tried not to fidget. Or tug at the collar of his shirt.

He was at a bloody art showing at Farley's gallery. He scanned the well-dressed crowd. He wasn't here to check the security, no, it was his bloody art on display.

He took a large chug of his beer. How the hell had he ever let Addie talk him into this?

She was sneaky. She'd slowly brought him around to the idea, and she damn well knew he couldn't say no to her.

Next to him, one of his carvings of Addie sat on a pedestal. All around the gallery, his statues were being hemmed and hawed over by strangers. He wasn't sure he liked it.

Addie had gently bullied him into showing his art to

Eamon. After that, things had moved at lightspeed, and here he was, having an art showing.

"Congratulations." Killian, wearing a dark suit and black shirt, appeared. His boss held up a glass of champagne in salute. "Please tell me you aren't going to quit Sentinel Security to become a full-time artist."

"Fuck, no. It's just a hobby." Apparently, no one ever listened when he said that.

"It's great work, Bram. You should be proud."

"Thanks." He took another sip of beer.

A familiar, sunshiny sound cut across the crowd. He turned his head. He'd know Addie's laugh anywhere. She was standing with Hex, Devyn, and Saskia. Her blue maternity dress covered the huge mound of her belly. She was due any day now, and he didn't think her stomach could possibly get any bigger. She had trouble sleeping at night, and he spent a lot of time rubbing her back.

Feck. The babies would arrive soon. He was both nervous and excited.

The nursery was ready now. Addie had loved every second of selecting the furniture, toys, and decorations.

Everything was ready, except for him.

"Bram! The show is fabulous." Eamon Farley appeared. The older Irishman was wearing a suit in an eye-searing pink color. He slapped Bram's arm. "Just *fabulous.*"

"Thanks," Bram rumbled.

Eamon looked at Killian. "The Irish. We have so many talents, and we're artistic souls." He slapped Bram's back.

Nearby, Bram spotted Nick, Matteo, and Shade. The

three men were grinning at him. The bastards. They were standing with Camden Morgan, who was also holding a beer.

"Now, I see some people are interested in buying the few pieces you've put up for sale. Let me go broker a good price for you." Eamon winked. "I'll have some good Irish whiskey ready for us to celebrate with." He swept off.

Bram fought the urge to tug at his collar.

"Addie looks happy," Killian said.

"Yeah, but the pregnancy has been tough on her the last few weeks. Over half of twin pregnancies have been delivered by now."

Killian squeezed his shoulder. "She's fine. She has a good doctor."

Bram just grunted. He let his gaze trace her face. Her hair was up tonight, baring her long, elegant neck. She glowed and did look happy.

Someone called out for Killian, and with a nod at Bram, he moved away.

Bram just kept watching his wife.

They'd married in a simple ceremony at City Hall, then had a party at *On the Rocks* to celebrate. Paddy had hired a great Irish band, and the whiskey had flowed all night.

Lately, Addie had done some contract work with Hex, helping with computer work at Sentinel Security, but she was also spending time putting together an online ballet course. She'd had a brilliant idea to combine all the things she liked.

Saskia was helping her and acting as a model in the videos. Addie was enjoying building the site, and putting the content together. Saskia was going to offer the course through her ballet school, but Addie had dreams to make the course available to everyone, including disadvantaged children who otherwise wouldn't be able to make it to expensive dance lessons.

She was really excited to do work she loved, and stay at home with the twins.

Hex said something and Addie laughed again. Bram found himself smiling. Yeah, life was pretty damn good. He knew his ma and Fiona would be happy for him. He'd even had a few calls with his father that weren't stilted and awkward. His da was actually excited to become a grandfather.

Devyn appeared at his side. "Now, don't panic."

Bram tensed.

"Addie's in labor," his friend said.

Blind panic washed over him. "What?"

"The babies are coming. She's having some contractions. Nothing to panic about yet, as they aren't too close together."

Bram swallowed and just stared at her.

Devyn shook her head. "Hey, you're a former special forces badass, remember? You've got this. I know you have a hospital bag in your truck because I helped her pack it."

"She'll be in pain. Giving birth is dangerous—"

"Women do it every day, big guy."

"I can't lose her," he whispered.

Devyn's face softened. "You won't. You're in the middle of the city, surrounded by excellent hospitals.

Now, take a deep breath, because you need to be her support, and get her to the hospital."

"Hospital. Right." He saw Addie was sitting in a chair, taking some deep breaths. Hex, Lainie, Gabbi, Hadley and Saskia were with her. Saskia was holding her hand and Hex was looking at her phone, timing the contractions, he guessed.

Shit, it was really happening.

Addie turned her head and met his gaze. She smiled at him.

The knot in his gut eased.

It was him and Addie. Together.

He knew everything would be all right.

ADDIE WAS SO TIRED. But it was a good tired.

She leaned back against the pillows on the hospital bed, and listened to a loud, angry cry from her son.

"You have a hungry little man here." The smiling nurse carried baby Murphy over and handed him to Addie. The woman helped her get him settled on her chest and latched on. Then he started to suck.

Addie smiled down at her baby. He had a sturdy little body and red hair, just like his daddy.

"There he goes." The nurse nodded. "How are you feeling?"

"I'm good, thanks."

Murphy had been born first through a natural delivery, but Fiona had gone into distress, and Addie had been rushed in for an emergency C-section. Everything had worked out fine, but she was sure Bram had been worried the entire time. Thankfully, she'd known the Sentinel Security gang had been with him.

She glanced over and smiled.

Bram sat in an armchair beside her bed, holding a sleeping Fiona in his arms. The baby had a big, pink bow over her red hair. Addie loved how tiny she looked in Bram's big arms. He stared down at his daughter in awe.

"Bram?"

He looked up at Addie, and his face warmed. He rose, carefully so he didn't wake Fiona, and because she knew he was still afraid he'd drop the babies. It never failed to amuse her that a man used to working with weapons and bombs was scared of a tiny baby.

"You look beautiful," he said.

"Liar." She knew she must look tired and wrung out.

"You do." His voice was sincere, and she knew he meant it.

God, she loved him.

"Your son is very hungry." She gently stroked Murphy's soft cheek where he suckled noisily.

Bram watched with avid interest. "If he's anything like me, he'll be hungry until he hits adulthood."

"Well, they both have your red hair." They'd have to wait to see if the twins had blue or green eyes.

"Thank you, Addie. For them." His voice filled with emotion. "For loving me."

She reached out and took his hand. "You never have to thank me for that. I was born to love you, Bram O'Donovan."

He bent over her and pressed his lips to hers. She kissed her husband and basked in his love.

She had a man who adored her, and now two beautiful, precious babies.

Yes, dreams could morph and change, but if you never gave up believing, they really did come true.

I hope you enjoyed Bram and Addie's story!

Sentinel Security continues with *Hex*, starring Jet "Hex" Adler and a certain CIA spy. Coming mid-June 2023.

For more action-packed romance, check out the first book in the **Billionaire Heists**, *Stealing from Mr. Rich* (Monroe and Zane's story). **Read on for a preview of the first chapter.**

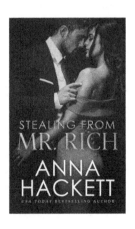

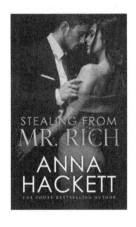

Brother in Trouble

Monroe

The old-fashioned Rosengrens safe was a beauty.

I carefully turned the combination dial, then pressed closer to the safe. The metal was cool under my fingertips. The safe wasn't pretty, but stout and secure. There was something to be said for solid security.

Rosengrens had started making safes in Sweden over a hundred years ago. They were good at it. I listened to the pins, waiting for contact. Newer safes had internals made from lightweight materials to reduce sensory feedback, so I didn't get to use these skills very often.

Some people could play the piano, I could play a safe. The tiny vibration I was waiting for reached my fingertips, followed by the faintest click.

"I've gotcha, old girl." The Rosengrens had quite a few quirks, but my blood sang as I moved the dial again.

I heard a louder click and spun the handle.

The safe door swung open. Inside, I saw stacks of jewelry cases and wads of hundred-dollar bills. *Nice.*

Standing, I dusted my hands off on my jeans. "There you go, Mr. Goldstein."

"You are a doll, Monroe O'Connor. Thank you."

The older man, dressed neatly in pressed chinos and a blue shirt, grinned at me. He had coke-bottle glasses, wispy, white hair, and a wrinkled face.

I smiled at him. Mr. Goldstein was one of my favorite people. "I'll send you my bill."

His grin widened. "I don't know what I'd do without you."

I raised a brow. "You could stop forgetting your safe combination."

The wealthy old man called me every month or so to open his safe. Right now, we were standing in the home office of his expensive Park Avenue penthouse.

It was decorated in what I thought of as "rich, old man." There were heavy drapes, gold-framed artwork, lots of dark wood—including the built-in shelves around the safe—and a huge desk.

"Then I wouldn't get to see your pretty face," he said.

I smiled and patted his shoulder. "I'll see you next month, Mr. Goldstein." The poor man was lonely. His wife had died the year before, and his only son lived in Europe.

"Sure thing, Monroe. I'll have some of those donuts you like."

We headed for the front door and my chest tightened. I understood feeling lonely. "You could do with some new locks on your door. I mean, your building has top-notch security, but you can never be too careful. Pop by the shop if you want to talk locks."

He beamed at me and held the door open. "I might do that."

"Bye, Mr. Goldstein."

I headed down the plush hall to the elevator. Every-thing in the building screamed old money. I felt like an imposter just being in the building. Like I had "daughter of a criminal" stamped on my head.

Pulling out my cell phone, I pulled up my accounting app and entered Mr. Goldstein's callout. Next, I checked my messages.

Still nothing from Maguire.

Frowning, I bit my lip. That made it three days since I'd heard from my little brother. I shot him off a quick text.

"Text me back, Mag," I muttered.

The elevator opened and I stepped in, trying not to worry about Maguire. He was an adult, but I'd practically raised him. Most days it felt like I had a twenty-four-year-old kid.

The elevator slowed and stopped at another floor. An older, well-dressed couple entered. They eyed me and my well-worn jeans like I'd crawled out from under a rock.

I smiled. "Good morning."

Yeah, yeah, I'm not wearing designer duds, and my bank account doesn't have a gazillion zeros. You're so much better than me.

Ignoring them, I scrolled through Instagram. When we finally reached the lobby, the couple shot me another dubious look before they left. I strode out across the marble-lined space and rolled my eyes.

During my teens, I'd cared about what people thought. Everyone had known that my father was Terry O'Connor—expert thief, safecracker, and con man. I'd felt every repulsed look and sly smirk at high school.

Then I'd grown up, cultivated some thicker skin, and learned not to care. *Fuck 'em.* People who looked down on others for things outside their control were assholes.

I wrinkled my nose. Okay, it was easier said than done.

When I walked outside, the street was busy. I smiled, breathing in the scent of New York—car exhaust, burnt meat, and rotting trash. Besides, most people cared more about themselves. They judged you, left you bleeding, then forgot you in the blink of an eye.

I unlocked my bicycle, and pulled on my helmet, then set off down the street. I needed to get to the store. The ride wasn't long, but I spent every second worrying about Mag.

My brother had a knack for finding trouble. I sighed. After a childhood, where both our mothers had taken off, and Da was in and out of jail, Mag was entitled to being a bit messed up. The O'Connors were a long way from the Brady Bunch.

I pulled up in front of my shop in Hell's Kitchen and stopped for a second.

I grinned. *All mine.*

Okay, I didn't own the building, but I owned the store. The sign above the shop said *Lady Locksmith*. The logo was lipstick red—a woman's hand with gorgeous red nails, holding a set of keys.

After I locked up my bike, I strode inside. A chime sounded.

God, I loved the place. It was filled with glossy, warm-wood shelves lined with displays of state-of-the-art locks and safes. A key-cutting machine sat at the back.

A blonde head popped up from behind a long, shiny counter.

"You're back," Sabrina said.

My best friend looked like a doll—small, petite, with a head of golden curls.

We'd met doing our business degrees at college, and had become fast friends. Sabrina had always wanted to be tall and sexy, but had to settle for small and cute. She was my manager, and was getting married in a month.

"Yeah, Mr. Goldstein forgot his safe code again," I said.

Sabrina snorted. "That old coot doesn't forget, he just likes looking at your ass."

"He's harmless. He's nice, and lonely. How's the team doing?"

Sabrina leaned forward, pulling out her tablet. I often wondered if she slept with it. "Liz is out back unpacking stock." Sabrina's nose wrinkled. "McRoberts overcharged us on the Schlage locks again."

"That prick." He was always trying to screw me over. "I'll call him."

"Paola, Kat, and Isabella are all out on jobs."

Excellent. Business was doing well. Lady Locksmith specialized in providing female locksmiths to all the single ladies of New York. They also advised on how to keep them safe—securing locks, doors, and windows.

I had a dream of one day seeing multiple Lady Locksmiths around the city. Hell, around every city. A girl could dream. Growing up, once I understood the damage my father did to other people, all I'd wanted was to be respectable. To earn my own way and add to the world, not take from it.

"Did you get that new article I sent you to post on the blog?" I asked.

Sabrina nodded. "It'll go live shortly, and then I'll post on Insta, as well."

When I had the time, I wrote articles on how women —single *and* married—should secure their homes. My latest was aimed at domestic-violence survivors, and helping them feel safe. I donated my time to Nightingale House, a local shelter that helped women leaving DV situations, and I installed locks for them, free of charge.

"We should start a podcast," Sabrina said.

I wrinkled my nose. "I don't have time to sit around recording stuff." I did my fair share of callouts for jobs, plus at night I had to stay on top of the business-side of the store.

"Fine, fine." Sabrina leaned against the counter and eyed my jeans. "Damn, I hate you for being tall, long, and gorgeous. You're going to look *way* too beautiful as my maid of honor." She waved a hand between us. "You're all tall, sleek, and dark-haired, and I'm...the opposite."

I had some distant Black Irish ancestor to thank for my pale skin and ink-black hair. Growing up, I wanted to be short, blonde, and tanned. I snorted. "Beauty comes in all different forms, Sabrina." I gripped her shoulders. "You are so damn pretty, and your fiancé happens to think you are the most beautiful woman in the world. Andrew is gaga over you."

Sabrina sighed happily. "He does and he is." A pause. "So, do you have a date for my wedding yet?" My bestie's voice turned breezy and casual.

Uh-oh. I froze. All the wedding prep had sent my normally easygoing best friend a bit crazy. And I knew very well not to trust that tone.

I edged toward my office. "Not yet."

Sabrina's blue eyes sparked. "It's only *four* weeks away, Monroe. The maid of honor can't come alone."

"I'll be busy helping you out—"

"Find a date, Monroe."

"I don't want to just pick anyone for your wedding—"

Sabrina stomped her foot. "Find someone, or I'll find someone for you."

I held up my hands. "Okay, okay." I headed for my office. "I'll—" My cell phone rang. *Yes.* "I've got a call. Got to go." I dove through the office door.

"I won't forget," Sabrina yelled. "I'll revoke your best-friend status, if I have to."

I closed the door on my bridezilla bestie and looked at the phone.

Maguire. Finally.

I stabbed the call button. "Where have you been?"

"We have your brother," a robotic voice said.

My blood ran cold. My chest felt like it had filled with concrete.

"If you want to keep him alive, you'll do exactly as I say."

Zane

God, this party was boring.

Zane Roth sipped his wine and glanced around the ballroom at the Mandarin Oriental. The party held the Who's Who of New York society, all dressed up in their glittering best. The ceiling shimmered with a sea of crystal lights, tall flower arrangements dominated the tables, and the wall of windows had a great view of the Manhattan skyline.

Everything was picture perfect...and boring.

If it wasn't for the charity auction, he wouldn't be dressed in his tuxedo and dodging annoying people.

"I'm so sick of these parties," he muttered.

A snort came from beside him.

One of his best friends, Maverick Rivera, sipped his wine. "You were voted New York's sexiest billionaire bachelor. You should be loving this shindig."

Mav had been one of his best friends since college. Like Zane, Maverick hadn't come from wealth. They'd both earned it the old-fashioned way. Zane loved numbers and money, and had made Wall Street his hunting ground. Mav was a geek, despite not looking like a stereotypical one. He'd grown up in a strong, Mexican-American family, and with his brown skin, broad shoulders, and the fact that he worked out a lot, no one would pick him for a tech billionaire.

But under the big body, the man was a computer geek to the bone.

"All the society mamas are giving you lots of speculative looks." Mav gave him a small grin.

"Shut it, Rivera."

"They're all dreaming of marrying their daughters off to billionaire Zane Roth, the finance King of Wall Street."

Zane glared. "You done?"

"Oh, I could go on."

"I seem to recall another article about the billionaire bachelors. All three of us." Zane tipped his glass at his friend. "They'll be coming for you, next."

Mav's smile dissolved, and he shrugged a broad shoulder. "I'll toss Kensington at them. He's pretty."

Liam Kensington was the third member of their trio. Unlike Zane and Mav, Liam had come from money, although he worked hard to avoid his bloodsucking family.

Zane saw a woman in a slinky, blue dress shoot him a welcoming smile.

He looked away.

When he'd made his first billion, he'd welcomed the attention. Especially the female attention. He'd bedded more than his fair share of gorgeous women.

Of late, nothing and no one caught his interest. Women all left him feeling numb.

Work. He thrived on that.

A part of him figured he'd never find a woman who made him feel the same way as his work.

"Speak of the devil," Mav said.

Zane looked up to see Liam Kensington striding toward them. With the lean body of a swimmer, clad in a perfectly tailored tuxedo, he looked every inch the billionaire. His gold hair complemented a face the ladies oohed over.

People tried to get his attention, but the real estate mogul ignored everyone.

He reached Zane and Mav, grabbed Zane's wine, and emptied it in two gulps.

"I hate this party. When can we leave?" Having spent his formative years in London, he had a posh British accent. Another thing the ladies loved. "I have a contract to work on, my fundraiser ball to plan, and things to catch up on after our trip to San Francisco."

The three of them had just returned from a business trip to the West Coast.

"Can't leave until the auction's done," Zane said.

Liam sighed. His handsome face often had him voted the best-looking billionaire bachelor.

"Buy up big," Zane said. "Proceeds go to the Boys and Girls Clubs."

"One of your pet charities," Liam said.

"Yeah." Zane's father had left when he was seven. His mom had worked hard to support them. She was his hero. He liked to give back to charities that supported kids growing up in tough circumstances.

He'd set his mom up in a gorgeous house Upstate that she loved. And he was here for her tonight.

"Don't bid on the Phillips-Morley necklace, though," he added. "It's mine."

The necklace had a huge, rectangular sapphire pendant surrounded by diamonds. It was the real-life necklace said to have inspired the necklace in the movie, *Titanic*. It had been given to a young woman, Kate Florence Phillips, by her lover, Henry Samuel Morley. The two had run away together and booked passage on the Titanic.

Unfortunately for poor Kate, Henry had drowned when the ship had sunk. She'd returned to England with the necklace and a baby in her belly.

Zane's mother had always loved the story and pored over pictures of the necklace. She'd told him the story of the lovers, over and over.

"It was a gift from a man to a woman he loved. She was a shop girl, and he owned the store, but they fell in love, even though society frowned on their love." She sighed. "That's true love, Zane. Devotion, loyalty, through the good times and the bad."

Everything Carol Roth had never known.

Of course, it turned out old Henry was much older than his lover, and already married. But Zane didn't want to ruin the fairy tale for his mom.

Now, the Phillips-Morley necklace had turned up, and was being offered at auction. And Zane was going to get it for his mom. It was her birthday in a few months.

"Hey, is your fancy, new safe ready yet?" Zane asked Mav.

His friend nodded. "You're getting one of the first ones. I can have my team install it this week."

"Perfect." Mav's new Riv3000 was the latest in high-tech safes and said to be unbreakable. "I'll keep the necklace in it until my mom's birthday."

Someone called out Liam's name. With a sigh, their friend forced a smile. "Can't dodge this one. Simpson's an investor in my Brooklyn project. I'll be back."

"Need a refill?" Zane asked Mav.

"Sure."

Zane headed for the bar. He'd almost reached it when a manicured hand snagged his arm.

"Zane."

He looked down at the woman and barely swallowed his groan. "Allegra. You look lovely this evening."

She did. Allegra Montgomery's shimmery, silver dress

hugged her slender figure, and her cloud of mahogany brown hair accented her beautiful face. As the only daughter of a wealthy New York family—her father was from *the* Montgomery family and her mother was a former Miss America—Allegra was well-bred and well-educated but also, as he'd discovered, spoiled and liked getting her way.

Her dark eyes bored into him. "I'm sorry things ended badly for us the other month. I was..." Her voice lowered, and she stroked his forearm. "I miss you. I was hoping we could catch up again."

Zane arched a brow. They'd dated for a few weeks, shared a few dinners, and some decent sex. But Allegra liked being the center of attention, complained that he worked too much, and had constantly hounded him to take her on vacation. Preferably on a private jet to Tahiti or the Maldives.

When she'd asked him if it would be too much for him to give her a credit card of her own, for monthly expenses, Zane had exited stage left.

"I don't think so, Allegra. We aren't...compatible."

Her full lips turned into a pout. "I thought we were *very* compatible."

He cleared his throat. "I heard you moved on. With Chip Huffington."

Allegra waved a hand. "Oh, that's nothing serious."

And Chip was only a millionaire. Allegra would see that as a step down. In fact, Zane felt like every time she looked at him, he could almost see little dollar signs in her eyes.

He dredged up a smile. "I wish you all the best, Allegra. Good evening." He sidestepped her and made a beeline for the bar.

"What can I get you?" the bartender asked.

Wine wasn't going to cut it. It would probably be frowned on to ask for an entire bottle of Scotch. "Two glasses of Scotch, please. On the rocks. Do you have Macallan?"

"No, sorry, sir. Will Glenfiddich do?"

"Sure."

"Ladies and gentlemen," a voice said over the loud-speaker. The lights lowered. "I hope you're ready to spend big for a wonderful cause."

Carrying the drinks, Zane hurried back to Mav and Liam. He handed Mav a glass.

"Let's do this," Mav grumbled. "And next time, I'll make a generous online donation so I don't have to come to the party."

"Drinks at my place after I get the necklace," Zane said. "I have a very good bottle of Macallan."

Mav stilled. "How good?"

"Macallan 25. Single malt."

"I'm there," Liam said.

Mav lifted his chin.

Ahead, Zane watched the evening's host lift a black cloth off a pedestal. He stared at the necklace, the sapphire glittering under the lights.

There it was.

The sapphire was a deep, rich blue. Just like all the photos his mother had shown him.

"Get that damn necklace, Roth, and let's get out of here," Mav said.

Zane nodded. He'd get the necklace for the one woman in his life who rarely asked for anything, then escape the rest of the bloodsuckers and hang with his friends.

Billionaire Heists

Stealing from Mr. Rich
Blackmailing Mr. Bossman
Hacking Mr. CEO

PREVIEW: NORCROSS SECURITY

W ant more action-packed romance? Then check out the men of **Norcross Security**.

The only man who can keep her safe is her boss' gorgeous brother.

Museum curator Haven McKinney has sworn off men. All of them. Totally. She's recently escaped a bad ex and started a new life for herself in San Francisco. She *loves* her job at the Hutton Museum, likes her new boss, and has made best friends with his feisty sister. Haven's also desperately trying *not* to notice their brother: hotshot investigator Rhys Norcross. And she's *really* trying not to notice his muscular body, sexy tattoos, and charming smile.

Nope, Rhys is off limits. But then Haven finds herself in the middle of a deadly situation...

Investigator Rhys Norcross is good at finding his targets. After leaving an elite Ghost Ops military team, the former Delta Force soldier thrives on his job at his brother's security firm, Norcross Security. He's had his eye on smart, sexy Haven for a while, but the pretty curator with her eyes full of secrets is proving far harder to chase down than he anticipated.

Luckily, Rhys never, ever gives up.

When thieves target the museum and steal a multi-million-dollar painting in a daring theft, Haven finds herself in trouble, and dangers from her past rising. Rhys vows to do whatever it takes to keep her safe, and Haven finds herself risking the one thing she was trying so hard to protect—her heart.

Norcross Security

The Investigator
The Troubleshooter
The Specialist
The Bodyguard
The Hacker

The Powerbroker
The Detective
The Medic
The Protector
Also Available as Audiobooks!

ALSO BY ANNA HACKETT

Blackmailing Mr. Bossman

Hacking Mr. CEO

Also Available as Audiobooks!

Team 52

Mission: Her Protection

Mission: Her Rescue

Mission: Her Security

Mission: Her Defense

Mission: Her Safety

Mission: Her Freedom

Mission: Her Shield

Mission: Her Justice

Also Available as Audiobooks!

Treasure Hunter Security

Undiscovered

Uncharted

Unexplored

Unfathomed

Untraveled

Unmapped

Unidentified

Undetected

Also Available as Audiobooks!

Oronis Knights

Knightmaster

Galactic Kings

Overlord

Emperor

Captain of the Guard

Conqueror

Also Available as Audiobooks!

Eon Warriors

Edge of Eon

Touch of Eon

Heart of Eon

Kiss of Eon

Mark of Eon

Claim of Eon

Storm of Eon

Soul of Eon

King of Eon

Also Available as Audiobooks!

Galactic Gladiators: House of Rone

Sentinel

Defender

Centurion

Paladin

Guard

Weapons Master

Also Available as Audiobooks!

Galactic Gladiators

Gladiator

Warrior

Hero

Protector

Champion

Barbarian

Beast

Rogue

Guardian

Cyborg

Imperator

Hunter

Also Available as Audiobooks!

Hell Squad

Marcus

Cruz

Gabe

Reed

Roth

Noah

Shaw

Holmes

Niko

Finn

Devlin

Theron

Hemi

Ash

Levi

Manu

Griff

Dom

Survivors

Tane

Also Available as Audiobooks!

The Anomaly Series

Time Thief

Mind Raider

Soul Stealer

Salvation

Anomaly Series Box Set

The Phoenix Adventures

Among Galactic Ruins

At Star's End

In the Devil's Nebula

On a Rogue Planet

Beneath a Trojan Moon

Beyond Galaxy's Edge

On a Cyborg Planet

Return to Dark Earth

On a Barbarian World

Lost in Barbarian Space

Through Uncharted Space

Crashed on an Ice World

Perma Series

Winter Fusion

A Galactic Holiday

Warriors of the Wind

Tempest

Storm & Seduction

Fury & Darkness

Standalone Titles

Savage Dragon

Hunter's Surrender

One Night with the Wolf

For more information visit www.annahackett.com

ABOUT THE AUTHOR

I'm a USA Today bestselling romance author who's passionate about ***fast-paced, emotion-filled*** contemporary romantic suspense and science fiction romance. I love writing about people overcoming unbeatable odds and achieving seemingly impossible goals. I like to believe it's possible for all of us to do the same.

I live in Australia with my own personal hero and two very busy, always-on-the-move sons.

For release dates, behind-the-scenes info, free books, and other fun stuff, sign up for the latest news here:

Website: www.annahackett.com

Made in the USA
Monee, IL
31 May 2023